C000283498

THE SILENT ARMY

Margaret Rogers

Compugraphic Design Publishing

First published in Great Britain in 2010
by Compugraphic Design Publishing

Copyright © 2010 Margaret Rogers

Compugraphic Design Publishing
41 Vallis Way,
FROME BA11 3BA

Cover design by Alan Rogers

The right of Margaret Rogers to be identified as the author of
this work has been asserted by her in accordance with the Copyright, Designs
and Patent Act 1988

All rights reserved. No part of this publication may be reproduced, stored in a
retrieval system, or transmitted by any means, without the prior permission
in writing of the author.

ISBN 978-0-9566367-0-6

This book is sold subject to the condition that it shall not, by
way or trade or otherwise, be lent, re-sold, hired out, or otherwise circulated
without the publisher's prior consent in any form of binding or cover other
than that in which it is published and without a similar condition including
this condition being imposed on the subsequent purchaser.

Typeset in Baskerville

This book is dedicated to

my late husband

Andrew John Rogers

and to the brave men and women

who served in the

Auxiliary Units

About the Author

Margaret Rogers was born in Southampton in 1919 and lived through the Blitz while working at Marks & Spencer's store, until her home was bombed, when she and her parents took their few remaining belongings and caught a bus to the New Forest town of Fordingbridge. Within a couple of years she married Andrew, a farmer in reserved occupation during the war. He was a member of the Home Guard but this was only a cover for his real role as a member of the Auxiliary, Churchill's secret army. He was trained in sabotage and how to kill silently, at Coleshill and his Unit had an underground bunker in the woods near Fordingbridge.

Margaret has loved writing all her life and has had a number of letters and short articles published over the years in various magazines, her first being in the Farmers Weekly during the 1950's. She has just finished writing this, her first full-length novel, drawing on her own experiences during the Southampton Blitz, and on her husband's activities within the Auxiliary Unit. She still lives in Fordingbridge and celebrated her 90th birthday in 2009.

Acknowledgements

I should like to thank the following people for their help, without whose encouragement and assistance this book would never have made it into print:

My son Alan who has acted as my publisher

His friend Philip Baskerville who typeset it for me

Alan, Suzanne and Jamie at Compugraphic Design who contributed to the cover design

Martin Cooper at Marlinzo Services who formatted the final draft ready for printing and gave so generously of his time and advice

All the characters in this book are fictitious and any resemblance to actual persons living or dead is purely coincidental.

"The Silent Army"

Margaret Rogers 2010

Southampton in the year 1940

Our defences were weak at that time and there was intense bombing by German planes all around Southampton and nearby towns. The final air-raid on the centre of the town left people numb with shock at the devastation, and frightened, with all our troops scattered abroad, fighting the Germans. We were very alone and vulnerable.

People in Britain feared one thing now: Invasion! Would the enemy land on our shores and capture this island? 'Not without a fight,' they said.

It didn't happen. But what would life here in this precious island have been like if Hitler's forces had invaded and occupied our country? This is the story of the humour, courage and inner strength of the ordinary working people, trying to run their lives with German soldiers around them every waking hour. This is what it could have been like.

Prologue

'I should go on home, Nurse. There's sure to be another air raid tonight.' Doctor Shaw smiled at Eileen.

She hurried out of the hospital and then on a sudden impulse, decided to go and meet Ann so that they could go home together. When she arrived at the big department store, they had already closed and Ann was walking down the road in front of her.

'Come on Sis,' muttered Eileen, 'we must hurry home. There's going to be another raid tonight.' Ann tucked her arm into her sister's and they made for the bus stop. Their home was just on the outskirts of Southampton. Half of the people of the town had the same idea. There was a queue at the bus stop, only now it was no longer a queue but a mass of frightened people. A group of workmen were fighting to get home to their loved ones. The girls knew that they were doomed. If they didn't get out of the town now, it would be too late. No buses would run during a raid.

Ann saw another double-decker bus coming round the corner. 'Come on, let's flag him down. Put your hand up Sis.' The bus braked quickly and let the girls on. Who would refuse two pretty young girls? With a sigh of relief Eileen said, 'Where's it going?' They waited for the conductress to come and take their fares but no one did.

The driver pulled up at the next stop and took on another load of passengers and it was then that Eileen heard the sirens blasting forth their ominous cry. The bus sped on for another few hundred yards and then the driver could hear the shrapnel coming down from the anti-aircraft guns so he braked hard and shouted, 'Get out you lot and run for a shelter!'

But there were no shelters, only a few modern-style houses which ran along the opposite side of the road. Eileen and Ann ran like hell, up to the front door of one and banged hard but there was no answer, so they tried the next one. This was more hopeful: There was a chink of light between the front room curtains and the radio could be heard going full belt. The first planes were coming over, dropping incendiaries to burn quickly and light up the town. They kept on banging until the door opened and a young woman, not much older than the girls, stood there, as if they were carol singers. She seemed not to have noticed the impending air-raid so they just pushed past her and let themselves in.

'Down to the shelter quick!' said Eileen.

'I didn't know there was a raid on,' the young woman said. 'I've just finished bathing my baby.'

The girls had never moved so quickly in their lives; Ann picked up the baby, lying on the table on towels, while Eileen carried all the gear for the baby's needs.

'How old's the baby?' asked Ann, as they all ran down the few steps to the gloomy Anderson shelter at the bottom of the garden.

'Eight weeks,' said the young mother, taking the baby and rocking her to and fro. 'I'm so glad you came to my door.' She was weeping now. 'I didn't know there was an air raid started. I had the radio on.'

'Yes, so we noticed. Have you no man about the house?'

'Yes, my husband's a policeman and he's on duty.'

'Try not to be frightened,' said Eileen. The atmosphere in the dark musty shelter was filled with foreboding and fear. All because of a tiny baby. The girls leaned across her as if their bodies would save her from harm.

Then it all started: Bombs began falling all around them; the noise was like something out of hell; the ground shook at times and now and then the bombs made a screaming sound. There was a shatter of breaking glass and a thump! 'That was my conservatory,' said the young woman, her voice high pitched with fear.

'That's too near,' Ann said, clutching her sister's arm. Eileen wrapped her arms around her twin.

Then for five minutes it went quiet. The door of the shelter opened and a young policeman was framed in the doorway. The young couple cuddled and cried and then in a flash he was gone again. Duty called. The short spell of peace was over. The bombers were back overhead again, releasing their objects of destruction and they were coming too near now. Heavy bombs were now the reason for the ground shaking. The aircraft were coming over in waves.

And so it continued all night until the morning light, which was not nature's reassuring glow but the ugly lamp of fire that made the sky so red that people could see it from the New Forest, five miles away. Groups of people watched in disbelief as the sky glowed redder every minute. When the last bomber had gone and the all-clear siren sounded in the early morning air, the girls left the shelter. The house was a mess, but more important than that, the baby was safe. It

3

was heartbreaking to have to leave them. They were all suffering from shock and the thing that worried Ann the most was the fact that their own mother had been alone that night.

As they picked their way through the rubble, the broken glass from some shop fronts and the tangle of telephone wires strewn across the road and over the pavement, it dawned on them. Was mum alright? The only way to find out was to get home as fast as they could!

It was the most difficult and heart-rending walk they had ever had. Unexploded bombs and large craters in the road, fires still burning and all the emergency services doing their best to rescue people who were trapped in the rubble. It took Ann and Eileen two hours to do a twenty minutes walk home, often having to make a detour when the mountains of rubble blocked their way completely. They found their mother in the shelter with her old friend and neighbour Ethel. The girls fell into her arms.

'Whatever next! Are you day dreaming again Nurse Smith?' Matron poked her finger in Eileen's shoulder blade. 'It's time you went round with the supper drinks and the bedpans.' Eileen got up from her chair and looked at the ward report in front of her. Good grief! She hadn't written a word. She had been going back over the past. It was no good. She mustn't let herself go down that path again. It was too horrible! Then losing her mum and her gran a few weeks later. It was stupid raking it all up again. That was all Jim Blake's fault, telling her that she didn't know what war was like. 'Wait till I get my hands on him,' Eileen thought. 'I'll tell him what Ann and I went through.' Her heart fluttered at the thought of seeing him. He was all right, Jim Blake.

Softly closing the back door behind him, Jim went round to the shed, opened the ferret cage and slipped his two ferrets in the deep inside pocket of his jacket and went out into the forest to get a rabbit. He trod quietly and the silence of the night was beautiful in the New Forest, with only the hoot of an owl, and the whisper of sound as a tiny night creature searched the dead winter leaves for food. Soon nature's system of birth and creation would begin again and the forest would grow its carpet and canopy of blossom and new life. Jim loved every bit of it. He was a Forrester by birth.

The moon was bright and a patch of light shone on the forest floor between the trees. Jim was thinking about the story of the black panther that people said had been seen in the Forest, when a pair of green eyes suddenly appeared a few yards away from him. It was one of the wild cats that made the Forest their home. Looking like a household pet, it was easy to mistake it, but the scratch or bite was something you never forgot if you touched it. Jim kept perfectly still. He knew it would be no use to let his ferrets go into a rabbit burrow now. He would not get a rabbit tonight; the cat had driven them away from the area. He decided that he would retrace his steps back to his cottage. Actually, he had walked further than he had ever meant to and he realised that he was deeper in the Forest than he usually went.

He was about to turn round when he saw the ground ahead of him move! Slowly an evergreen bush and clump of bramble rose upwards. Jim rubbed his eyes and lay flat on his face until he could take a hold of himself. His heart was beating so fast it was disturbing the little ferrets which now were round his neck inside his shirt.

Suddenly without warning a man scrambled out of a hole in the ground and slowly lowered the forest carpet down, like a lid, to normal again.

Jim rose to his feet and watched as the man gently trod the ground around him, covering the entrance to the hole. He brushed his clothing with a bare hand and taking a pistol from his pocket, checked it and put it back. Turning round slowly, the simply-dressed farm labourer scanned the silent forest and it was then that he saw Jim, now crouching half behind a bush. Like a flash, his hand went to his pocket for the gun but Jim was swifter and dropped down sideways into the tangled undergrowth, just as a bullet whined past his sleeve. For a terrifying moment Jim thought a second one would now kill him, as the rustle of dry, dead leaves gave his position away. He did the only thing he could do now: He shouted. 'It's Jim Blake! From Beech Cottage.'

Silence again. He felt clammy with sweat. The forest was full of dark patches. Then the moon slipped behind a cloud and the circle of light between the leafless trees was gone. He got to his feet and held his hands up, his eyes trying to pierce the blackness but couldn't see the man with the pistol.

He stood there for what seemed an eternity. It was so quiet. He could have been alone in the forest. Not a twig or leaf stirred. Then a gentle tap on his back made him jump. The shock alone could have killed him and he made to turn round to see who had crept up behind him, when suddenly there was an arm around his neck and a knife at his throat, as a muffled voice barked at him, 'Don't turn around, Jim. You must not see me nor discover my identity. If you do, then I have orders to kill you. You're a bloody fool. You've seen something you should never have seen. I wish you hadn't. No! Don't move, or try to see me. Just listen. I could get shot myself for telling you this. But the reason why I'm going to trust you is because you're a close friend of Ray Wicks. You don't know me, but he told me once to trust you. Trust you with his life. Well, Jim, you've accidentally come upon the secret hideaway of the local resistance movement, the Auxiliary. There are hundreds of us just in the south area. Here, and Ringwood, and places all over the south of England. We were all trained by the army for a German invasion, should it come. When they arrive, and you know as well as us, it could be any day, we'll be ready for them, ready to start killing them and disrupting their movements. We shall probably have a short life but a merry one and we'll take a lot of them with us. Now, Jim, about the army secret: You must swear on your life that you will never repeat what I'm telling you.'

Jim stood tall and the moon came again through a gap in the trees and shone on him. It was strange, terrifying almost.

'I swear on everything I hold dear to me. I swear on oath that what went on tonight is no more. Wiped out, never ever to pass my lips.'

'Right,' said the man behind him. 'Now get going Jim, and don't look back. And put those bloody ferrets in a pocket!'

'How did you know?' said Jim.

'We're trained to spot things under a man's shirt,' he replied with a grin.

Jim lingered about in his own garden when he got back to the cottage. He set a couple of snares down near the fence and hoped for a rabbit in the morning. When he went into the kitchen there was a note on the table. 'Gone on to bed, love Mum.'

He made himself a hot drink and washed the dust from his hair and face at the kitchen sink. He didn't want to wake his mother. Desperately tired, he went to bed. But sleep didn't come. He was still in the forest, still there among the dark, tall trees, waiting for the second bullet and wondering what death was like. His thoughts turned to Eileen. He would go and see her tomorrow. Then he realised that it was already tomorrow, it was four-thirty in the morning!

Chapter 1

Eileen and Ann Smith were twenty two years old and identical twins, both tall and beautiful with dark hair which they both wore in the fashion of the time, the Page-boy bob. They used no make-up on their pale skins at the request of their mother, who was now gone, killed during an air-raid only eight weeks before. She had been on a visit to the twins' granny and they were out shopping together when the bomb had hit the square and market place.

The twins were still grieving for their mother and granny. They were living on their own in the little Edwardian house that had belonged to their parents. Their father had died when the girls were small children and in fact, they had difficulty in remembering him. Life had revolved around their mother.

Eileen was a nurse and worked in the General Hospital nearby. She loved the work. Ann worked in one of the large department stores, on the counter. She was now out of a job as the long row of shops had been bombed, including the one where she had worked. At the moment she was working at the local junior school, where they now made parachutes for the war-effort. The school had been taken over for war work as the children had all been evacuated to safer places in the country villages around the New Forest.

Eileen had many friends among the nursing staff, including a young doctor by the name of John Shaw. He was in love with her but he was not the one for Eileen: He was too reserved, she was full of fire and passion.

Ann had few friends. She was shy and a dreamer, quiet when at the little factory. They called her 'Little mouse', though she was far from small.

Eileen had one boyfriend, though he was no longer a boy. He was thirty, unmarried and a train driver. He had been in the hospital where she worked. An accident at work had not been serious but Eileen had got to know him in the ward as his burns were treated. He had grown fond of her and suffered the badly burned leg in silence, except to tell her that he was single and that his name was Jim Blake. He worked on the Southampton to Waterloo line each day. A trained and skilled engine driver, he had always had a passion for trains. His mate, Bob Stick, the fireman, was younger and at eighteen, was awaiting his call-up to join the army, which would be so different to shovelling coal into the furnace of the huge steam locomotive.

It was not entirely Bob's fault that his mate the driver, Jim Blake had been burned. The express train had been forced to brake violently. The single German plane had dropped a bomb on the line ahead, missing the bridge across the line but causing a huge crater.

Jim had told Eileen that he had never been so scared in his life, to which Eileen had replied curtly that had he lived in Southampton, he would have known all about bombs. She had told him that his life in a country cottage where he lived with his widowed mother had obviously spoiled his outlook on real life. His village in the New Forest was not exactly a prime target. He had frowned at her and his eyes were as cold as steel. His hand had shot out from beneath the bed covers and grabbed hers. His voice was heavy with anger. 'If you care to take a trip up to London, you will no doubt learn when to keep your mouth shut. Londoners have been to hell and back,' he said. 'You're the one who knows nothing about bombs.'

Eileen tried hard over the next few weeks to erase those words from her mind. Unhappy and tired of wearing a false smile on her lips, she thought it was the end of their friendship, especially when she was placed on a new emergency ward and her time was too full to see him. Unable to get to speak to him, she wept at the empty bed. Her sister tried hard to change her mood. Both girls were still in mourning for their mother and granny. Ann said that she was sure he would find her before he left the hospital.

Jim Blake healed quickly, at least in the flesh. He asked Matron if he could have a few moments of her time before he was discharged. His yearning to see her and apologise was obvious to the staff. She granted him his request and asked him to follow her to her office. Matron was quite aware of the friendship that had come about from nursing this nice young man. She was also quite gifted at reading the character behind the nurse's uniform. Eileen was a good nurse. Matron had issued instructions for Eileen to wait outside her office until sent for.

When Jim Blake entered Matron's sanctuary, she called Eileen in. Both had stood, slightly embarrassed, as Matron pushed her chair out and sat down. She eased the tension by saying to her top nurse that this gentleman, Mr Blake, had wished to thank her nurses, especially nurse Smith, for her excellent care and attention.

Jim had shifted his feet and clung tightly to the crutch he had been given, wondering just when he had made that remark. He had smiled and inwardly thanked his good luck to have been in a hospital where the Matron had a soft heart.

Eileen had felt her heart thumping as she made her usual reply to a patient's gratitude. Her whole body shook as she glanced at Jim. To meet his eyes on her. For that one brief moment she knew he was in love with her. Cross words were only a forgotten pin-prick in time. Matron's voice stabbed at the silence as she dismissed the pair of them, firmly instructing Jim Blake to keep a light dressing on the leg for a few more days.

As they went out of the office together she told Eileen crisply to see Mr Blake to his taxi and be back on the ward in ten minutes. 'Time for Mr Blake to have a quick cup of tea,' she said carefully. Then she muttered, 'You can go back to work in a week's time, Mr Blake.'

Once outside, Jim reached for her hand and squeezed it. Together they walked around to the canteen where he took her in his arms, quietly unconscious of the noise, of the rattle of the teacups or the hiss of the hot-water boiler.

'I'd love to see you again,' Eileen said.

Doctor John Shaw was just passing through the entrance hall of the hospital and saw them both. He walked quickly to Victoria Ward. His finely chiselled face changed to a scowl and his mouth set in a fine line of tension, yet sadness too. He would have to win her back from that common-looking man, he vowed. They had only been out together a few times. They had been to the cinema and had seen a couple of dreary films together then had tea and hot crumpets in the corner cafe.

'Perhaps I've been too slow,' he pondered. 'Maybe if I ask her back to the flat we could browse through my sepia snap shots and then have a drink.' He was whisked out of his day-dreaming by a trolley heading straight for him. 'Doctor!' a voice warned him just and only just in time.

'So sorry, nurse.' He put on his charming smile and quickly glided through a half-open door to the men's ward.

Ann put the key into the door of number seven in Glenmore Road and let herself in. The small Edwardian house, out of eight in a row, was the home that she shared with her twin sister Eileen. The home they had grown up in struck her cold. She went straight into the kitchen, took off her coat and thick woollen scarf, then, throwing her purse on to the scrubbed wooden top table, she stared at the cold black kitchen range. A lump of emotion came into her throat. The old stove looked neglected and ugly, squat there, almost a stranger. Mum would have had a fire lit and a kettle singing away on the top. It used to shine black and red and they would sit and fight over slices of dripping toast.

Tears welled up in her eyes as she pictured the rice puddings with golden brown skin on the top, the stews in the big black pot, with dumplings on the top surface waiting to melt in your mouth.

'You've got more than me!' Ann would always cry.

Then mum banged the old table with her fist! 'Stop it you girls. You have two each!'

Ann slumped down in her chair and put her hands over her face. It was so cold and dreary in the kitchen.

'Oh mum, why did you leave us?' she whispered. Then she wiped away the tears that ran down her cheeks and knew that she had to carry on with life. 'For one thing, the damned room will never get warm unless I light the fire,' she muttered to herself.

Daylight was already fading and it was only four o'clock. Still, what could you expect, it was the first of December. Staring out of the kitchen window she saw something that made her smile and her mood changed: Her next door neighbour's clothes line had caught her eye. Mrs Sharpe had her apron on the line and it was as stiff as a board. The two ribbon ties were standing out like walking sticks each side, pointing to the ground. 'Well if it falls off the line it will stand up by itself, on its own two legs,' she smiled to herself.

It was a reminder to her to take her own apron from where it was hanging on the back of the kitchen door. It was time to get this fire lit and a meal prepared for herself and her sister. First there was a bucket of coal to get in from the outside bunker.

The coalman had been while they were at work. He had left a sackful of coal, some of it big lumps which would need breaking up. Ann picked up the piece of paper that was on the top. It read, 'Two shillings and sixpence. R.M.Pickles Coal Merchant.' On the back of the bill was a message. It was only a few words but it struck fear in her heart.

'Shortage. No more coal, coke or wood until the first of Jan. Sorry!'

Ann made her way back to the kitchen, her thoughts spinning inside her head. She was going to light the fire in the best room for Christmas: Would the fuel last until the end of the month, she wondered? Glancing at the clock on the shelf above the stove, she hurried to get things going, as it was a quarter to five according to the 'corned beef tin'. That was what her mum had always called it. They had had the clock for a couple of years now. It was tin! In fact, it had been full of toffees one Christmas, special offers from the local grocer shop in East Street. Eileen had bought it for mum from them both.

'Don't expect it will go!' her mum had snapped. 'Waste of money.' But the girls had wound it up and stood it on the shelf. It had never let them down, ticking away strongly even when the house had shaken from the land-mine bomb, dropped by parachute by German planes dropped at the end of their road in November.

Ann was still thinking about it as she cooked their tea. The half empty fish shop had let Eileen have two whale steaks, as fish was scarce. It was better than nothing at all, but Ann didn't really fancy it. Then she thought of the fishermen risking their lives to feed people.

She dished up the meal and placed the two plates on the bottom shelf of the oven. Eileen would soon be home from work. It will be nice to have company, thought Ann. She had done night shift at the hospital all last week. From today, she should be home by six o'clock.

She hated the nights alone when Eileen was on duty. Their next door neighbour Mrs Sharpe would sometimes come round for the evening, arriving with the same things each time: A pair of spectacles in a brown case with her late husband's initials on the top, a packet of Star brand cigarettes which never left her pocket all evening, and her knitting. The large ball of wool was khaki in colour and she was all intent on making gloves or socks for the soldiers. The Women's Institute supplied the wool. Ann had wondered when they would see the finished garment but they never did. Quite often Emily Sharpe would drop off to sleep and the ball of wool would roll off her lap and disappear under a chair.

'I nearly fell asleep,' she would say, with an almost toothless grin before she settled her dancing dentures back in place. Then Eileen or Ann would get on their knees and retrieve the ball of wool before making her a cup of cocoa. The urge to return home followed and she soon left.

Emily Sharpe had been a good friend of their mum's, so they tried hard to make her feel welcome: She had been a great help to them when it came to the funerals of granny and of their dear mother. The girls had been lost and Mrs Sharpe had arranged it for them, giving them love and support.

Ann sat in mum's rocking chair and began to get a little anxious: Eight o'clock and still Eileen has not come home. It was not like her. She always came home first when she had a date. Boyfriends over the years had always been willing to wait while she changed out of her nurse's uniform. 'They'll wait all day if they have to, for a girl like her!' mum used to say, with pride. But mum's final warning as they left the house never changed. She would point a finger at the pair of them and snap, 'No funny business mind!'

Eileen always resented it but Ann was far too shy and she lost opportunities with male friends. Many a parent was known to say, 'She thinks she's too good for my lad, that Smith girl.' Sometimes Ann heard them but she knew she couldn't change.

Ann found that evening depressing. She had eaten her half-cold meal and as the oven was cooling down she took her plate out to the tiny scullery where a cold water tap hovered sullenly over an old brown earthenware sink. The water was icy cold so she quickly rinsed her plate in the enamel bowl and went back to the warm kitchen. She had only just sat down when she heard it. There was a tapping on the connecting wall. Ann knew at once that it was Mrs Sharpe. Wondering what she wanted, Ann hurried to the back door.

Mrs Sharpe stood shivering in the night air. 'George has not come home for his tea and I did a nice hot stew too,' she muttered. 'Something's up! It's the war,' she said.

'Come in the warm. Don't stand there.' Ann took her arm and led her into the kitchen.

'He may be just working overtime.' Ann tried to sound cheerful. George was Mrs Sharpe's only son. He was a welder and worked in the docks. Of course, after the death of her husband George was the apple of his mother's eye.

'No.' She shook her head. 'He said only last night that there is not much work at the moment due to the last lot of bombing. Three of the yards were damaged – tools, welding stuff.'

On impulse, Ann gave her a hug. Her thin body was shaking. 'He'll be all right, you'll see,' she told her, going to the teapot. The tea was fresh as she had only just made it for herself. 'Have a cup of tea with me Emily.' Ann used her Christian name. 'Eileen has not come home yet either. She's late.'

'Oh my God! I told you something's up! I'll go back now Ann. I don't think I will stop for the tea in case he comes in. George will worry finding the empty house. It's them fifth-columnist lot! George said they nabbed two of them in the dockyard yesterday. German spies, Ann. German spies.' She hurried out.

As the back door opened, a gust of freezing air swept in. There was ice on the window. Ann felt sorry for her as she had a habit of playing make-believe. There was the time when she had reported a spy creeping about in the back garden. The poor air-raid warden was shocked and embarrassed when the police took him away for questioning. Emily couldn't show her face for days after that. Although she was wrong and felt foolish, she still said to the girls, 'I knew something was up!'

Ann put some coal on the fire. It was getting late to do this but Eileen would be cold when she did come home. She knew her sister was all right. It was a link between them, being twins. When Ann was ill or distressed, Eileen always knew and felt the same pain or discomfort.

She relaxed after a while, knowing that she wouldn't sleep if she went to bed. She spent the next few hours sitting quietly in her mother's rocking chair, a thing she took great comfort in. Kicking off her shoes, she gazed at the rag rug which they had made together. The corner was curled back and she could see a sample of the lino beneath. It was such a pretty green with yellow leaves scattered in a spring-like pattern. Preserved under the rug for so many years, it only made the faded, cracked lino around it look worse than ever. Everything in the kitchen was shabby, she thought sadly. The old kitchen table with its white wood top had not been scrubbed for ages.

Her eyes glanced across at the dresser. It was grubby and someone, at some time, had painted it brown. The paint was flaking off – she hadn't noticed that before. The tea-set with the blue and white pattern was nice. A man had once told her mum that it was Victorian and worth a few pounds if she wished to sell it. She had said no, very sternly and showed him the door. Their ration books were on the dresser. Ann took them and went through the coupons to see what they had left. The cheese dish was empty and there was no butter left. Eileen would have to get some sandwiches in the hospital canteen tomorrow.

She suddenly felt tired. Looking up at the clock, she was surprised to see that it was eleven fifteen. Ann went into the little front room to check before she went to bed. It was only a small room. A sofa against the wall covered in gingery brown plush. It had been Aunt Mary's. Two armchairs, one each side of the fireplace. These were covered in brown leather, almost out of place in such humble surroundings. The chairs were special and rarely used except on Christmas Day when the fire was lit. Much fuss had been made when her mother's only sister, Mary had died, leaving them and the china figure of Garibaldi on the mantle shelf, to her. Aunt Mary had married a wealthy businessman Herbert Walls, but no one ever knew what his business was. He was devious. He had left her after a few years and disappeared, never to be seen again. They were beautiful chairs and they possibly came from a gentleman's club. The girls never sat in them.

Ann turned the light off and, pulling the faded pink curtains aside looked out of the window at the road. It was so quiet that it felt creepy. Just a couple of men walking by, heading for the top of the road. They didn't make a sound so they must have been wearing shoes, not boots, Ann thought. Their long dark overcoats were glistening with frost. It was a bitter cold night, without street-lights. Ann went slowly up the stairs to the little back bedroom and so to bed. Eileen had her key.

She soon drifted off to sleep even though the bedroom was so cold. There was a fine sliver of ice on the jug of water standing on the wash stand. There was no bathroom in the house but there was a flush toilet downstairs with a door leading off the scullery to it. Most winters the pipes froze in the toilet as well as the main water tap over the sink. Her dreams didn't take that road to domestic problems. Hers centred on her work, work which she didn't like. There had been rumours lately that the works would be moving to a larger building. Would she have to go or move with them far away? It had caused her concern now for several days. The women she worked with were friendly and nice to her but knew little about the move. They had paid her a great compliment when they had said, 'We're taking Little Mouse with us, if we have to move!' A chorus of 'Yeah!' had left Ann in tears.

She tossed and turned in bed, but she slept. She slept all night. When she emerged from sleep at seven o'clock in the morning it was still dark. She made her way down to the kitchen and switched on the light. On the kitchen table was her sister's battery torch and beside it lay her keys, scarf, coat and gloves.

Eileen was home.

Chapter 2

Eileen watched as the taxi drew away. Jim Blake gave her a
huge grin as she said her goodbye. He was going home to his
mother in the Forest, to Beech Cottage but it was not home
that he was thinking about at that moment. It was victory in
the smile and the promise she made of her consent to them
spending time together.

As the taxi took him to the Forest hamlet that had been
his home all of his life, he could still see her lovely face and
feel her soft moist lips on his.

Eileen walked back to the Ward. Matron stood at the end
of the ward talking to the two elderly women patients sitting
out in chairs as they were getting ready to go home. She
turned to have a word with Eileen.

'Nurse Smith. Will you see that these two ladies have a
bath before they go home? Oh, and see they have warm
clothes on as it's freezing outside. By the way, have they got
family? I never see anyone visit. Get on to a charity if things
are poor. Salvation Army or their church. Find out if the
older one is a catholic. Maybe Father Walsh will help.'

'Yes Matron.' Eileen hesitated before asking why the
Ward Sister was not administering this home service. It was
her place to do so when the patient left the hospital with
after-care problems.

Matron read her thoughts: As she turned to go she said,
'Sister Fry is confined to her bed with influenza. I take it
that you will step in and fill her place for a short spell.'

'Of course, Matron.'

'Thank you, Nurse.'

Eileen carried on with her duties in the ward until 5:30 then she sat at her desk to make out her report. She was just about to sign off duty when the sound of running feet and voices in the corridor made her go out to see what was happening.

Matron was outside the ward. 'Make room in Men's Ward for three adult male patients. Emergency,' she barked.

Eileen joined the House Doctor, Dr Preston and the male nurse who were pushing two extra beds in the ward. After much pushing and manoeuvring they made room for the three extra beds.

Eileen obeyed rules and left the ward as the men were undressed and put into the waiting beds. However, she did notice when they came in that they all wore the same roll-neck navy jerseys and navy serge trousers.

'Fishermen,' she said to Dr Preston when she returned to her ward.

He gave her a look of disbelief. 'I can't understand it, Nurse. They can certainly swim, but the icy sea tonight! It's a wonder they got out alive. Will you get the basket trolley? Their wet clothes can go to the drying room.'

'Yes Doctor.' Eileen looked at the wet floor around the pile of clothes and added, 'Can I have the identification list please, to do their charts?'

'They have none,' he answered. 'In fact, not one of them has a name, number or a single mark on any of their clothes or underwear and nothing in their pockets. They are suffering from exposure at the moment. Later when they are stabilised I'll have to ask them some questions. We should have information about the ship which they were on. I wonder who brought them in.'

Eileen didn't have long to wait for an answer: Matron entered the ward. 'The Coastguard has just left. Duty done. Nurse Smith, would you be prepared to continue duty and work the night shift? I need a good nurse here. These men are suffering from exposure.'

She didn't answer at once. Matron read her thoughts: It was Sister Jones' place to do these tasks, Eileen was thinking. 'We are short staffed. Sister Jones has retired to her bed with influenza.' Matron actually smiled at Eileen.

'Yes, certainly I will sign on for her tonight,' she said.

Matron looked relieved at her answer and said quietly, 'I've a great respect for our fishermen.' She gave another half smile at her nurse and swept out of the ward, leaving her and Dr. Preston to nurse these rather unusual fishermen, who were now asleep. Or were they?

Eileen watched the men through the night. Dr Preston was on duty with her and was not happy at the situation. He whispered to her that he hadn't heard a word from them. They had all been examined and in his opinion they had not been in the sea very long, according to the tests done on their skin.

'There is something just not right, Nurse Smith,' he said softly. 'Do you think they are genuine?'

'I'll find out if they are really asleep doctor.'

'How? I've tried several times,' he said.

'Well now,' Eileen whispered, 'I'm just going to pop down to the canteen for a moment if that's all right ?'

'Will you bring me some tea please Nurse!' He had raised his voice now.

Eileen found the canteen occupied by two of the nurses from the Women's Ward. They recognised her and talked while she made two cups of tea.

'Have you any pepper?' she asked. They giggled and pointed to the tray of condiments.

'Good heavens girl. What do you want pepper for?'

Eileen smiled. 'To pep up this canteen tea,' she said, laughing. She picked up a small pepper pot together with the teas and left the nurses staring after her in amazement, as she made her way back to the ward.

There was an almost eerie silence as she walked along the dimly lit corridors. The Men's Ward was so quiet that her entrance back through the swing doors was the only sound. Dr Preston was seated at the desk in the middle of the room. He accepted the tea with a brief nod as he was writing his reports. She watched him start to drink it and said in a clear voice, 'Would you like a shake of sugar?'

'No, thank you,' he murmured, looking up. He was wondering what on earth she was doing with a pepper pot. Her eyes warned him not to ask. She turned towards the desk with her back to the beds. The three men faking sleep were cut off from the top of the ward by a dividing curtain. The male nurse was on duty in the other half with patients who had been admitted a week ago.

To the doctor's amazement, she carefully shook a little of the pepper on to the palm of her left hand and closed it quickly. Then in a clear but quiet voice she said to him, 'Shall I do my rounds of the patients now, Doctor Preston?'

He was a trifle mystified but answered, 'Yes Nurse Smith. It think it's time we did, although I can see they are all sleeping.'

In two of the beds she noticed an eyelid flicker. She opened her left hand and brushed it lightly across her chin. Dr Preston was feeling the pulse of the man who had given them most concern. He was satisfied now. In fact, he was just about to say so when Nurse Smith sneezed. The sneeze was followed by another. The sudden impact on the man was impossible to ignore. The three men jerked up from the pillows but could not sit up as their bodies were each wrapped tightly in a large woollen blanket, pinning their arms. They did not show signs of coming out of sleep. Their eyes held fear as they stared at the nurse and the doctor.

'I'm so sorry Doctor.'

'Put a handkerchief to your mouth when you do that Nurse,' Doctor Preston said sharply. 'Oh and get a tray and remove these cups from the bedsides.'

Nurse Smith picked up the tray with their cups on left on the desk, and the pepper pot and gathered up the rest of the cups. As she left the ward she was thinking, 'Who were these men?' Her nursing instinct told her that their symptoms were unlike those of hypothermia patients which she had dealt with in the past. The one to ask a few questions was the doctor in the Casualty Bay, the one who had sent the three patients up to Men's Ward for one night. He must have taken their pulse, noted skin colour and the need of a warm drink with ample sugar in. Their sugar level would be very low if they had hypothermia.

Another thing crossed her mind: How were the men going to manage without Ration Books or money? One of them had a watch – she had surprised him as he had put it under his pillow when they were getting into bed. Apart from that personal object not one of them had anything in their pockets. Strange! No money, wallets or photos of loved ones at home. So unlike fishermen. If that is what they were, she thought. Eileen had a strange feeling about them.

At three o'clock Doctor Preston softly pulled back the dividing curtain, bringing the two sections together. Male Nurse George West took Doctor Preston on a silent round of the beds: Most of the elderly patients were asleep. Their charts showed a gradual improvement. All the patients were doing fine and there was no need for concern. This was the dominating factor in Dr Preston leaving the ward. He signed off and told Nurse Smith that he was going to have a sleep and would be back in the morning at 6 o'clock. He would come straight here to Men's Ward and get these fishermen dressed.

Before he went out of the door he said to George and Nurse, 'Now, if they give you any trouble,' pointing to the three beds, 'ring at once for Matron and she will deal with them, be they fishermen or Neville Chamberlain. Her arms are like steel. You don't cross Matron, you know!'

It was four thirty when Matron came into the ward. Quite un-announced, her stiffly starched uniform breaking the silence. She went to the beds of the registered patients, silently studying their charts, and then she went across to the fishermen. They were all awake and stared solemnly at her. She didn't utter a sound but the long penetrating look which she gave them, enlarged their desire to get out of the hospital as soon as dawn broke.

Eileen was writing reports when she came across to her. She put down her pen and stood to attention – you did that as Nurse Grade One; only Sister would have remained seated. She wondered if Dr Preston had reported her about the pepper. But Matron gave her one of her half-smiles that were usually interpreted to mean, 'You, nurse, are not a bad worker. Keep it up!'

When she spoke it was crisp but somehow kind. 'You can sign off duty at five o'clock, Nurse Smith. It's early morning. You should go at six but you've been on your feet all night as well as on your previous shift, two until six. You can go! I don't want yet another of my nurses ill. We have three with this flu now. Thank you Eileen for standing in when there is an emergency.'

For just a moment Eileen stood still. Then Matron was gone. George stood with open mouth.

'God, she was butter and cream with you,' he remarked.

'Yes, she can be, George. But that's just the time to be on your guard. She has been known to follow up those kinds of remarks with, 'The cuffs on your uniform are filthy, Nurse. Go and change them.' I've got to know her,' Eileen said, with just a glimmer of fondness in her voice.

On her way home from the hospital, Eileen faced the crisp empty streets. Just a policeman plodding along, keeping well away from the bombed shops and houses which were only shells but could be dangerous with the few unexploded bombs that were always somewhere after a raid. Eileen realised that there had now been several nights without an air-raid. It was a treat to have the quiet nights and the feeling of safety. There had been an odd one in the daylight hours and she wondered about those. No bombs, just the soul-destroying noise of the ack-ack battery in the side street. It was better if you were in a shelter: The little bits of hot metal coming back down like hailstones could be lethal. Air-raid Wardens and the Home Guard came out on duty on the streets and on the roofs of buildings at night.

Eileen heard the sharp voice of a Home Guard on duty. He asked her what her name was, then, shining his torch on her, recognised the young Nurse Smith who his mother knew.

It was freezing cold and with the black-out in force it was not easy with only her tiny torch to see the edge of the pavement or a lamp-post rearing up out of the blackness.

'Keep your torch down,' he said. 'If there's an enemy plane about, he can see even the glow of a lighted cigarette. Funny hour for you to be leaving the hospital!'

'Well, no not really,' she said. 'I'm only an hour early. I've done a long night and Matron said I could go off duty at five o'clock this morning. Actually I did the extra shift because we had fishermen casualties. Three of them, brought in last night.'

The Home Guard had been walking along with her but now stopped abruptly. 'Fishermen! Where the hell had they been fishing? The Solent is out of bounds, Cowes Roads, Channel too.'

'I don't know,' she snapped. She was tired and he was god enough to walk alongside of her with his large torch. She was sorry that she had spoken harshly to him.

As they walked along she told him the whole story about the fishermen and Dr Preston, even the bit about the pepper. When she got to the bit about the watch that one of them had under his pillow, he laughed. 'Trust you to see it. You don't miss a trick!'

'Well,' she went on, 'I looked at the watch because it was an hour fast so I put it right for him. He was asleep or pretending to be. There was something a little different about the watch. The figure eleven caught my eye. It looked more like a tiny cross with three little gold dots painted on it. Actually it was so small I guess you wouldn't notice it but my eyes are pretty good.'

Eileen suddenly heard him breathe quickly and stop. 'This is twice you have stopped,' she said. 'I shall never get home at this rate Mr Clark.'

'Bill,' he said, 'call me Bill.'

'What is it?' she asked.

'My God, Eileen Smith. I hope you are wrong in what you saw on that watch. It is almost impossible anyhow!'

'Why?' She sensed something genuine in his manner, so asked him again, 'Why, what's wrong?'

'Well Eileen, there is only one watch in the world like that. Believe me girl, there could never be another. I asked the time one day of an old mate of mine and he lifted his left hand and showed me his watch so I could see the time. I thanked him and he was silent, deep in thought for a minute then he said quietly he'd let me into a little secret. He didn't tell people unless they had noticed and asked to look at it again. The eleven was for the eleventh of November. He had had three older brothers who he had adored, killed in the First World War. So when he grew up he had got a friend of his to make a special face for the watch to remember them by. The little tiny cross in the place where the number eleven should have been had to be nine-carat gold with three tiny dots of gold on it to represent his three brothers. The remaining numerals were also done in gold.' Bill's voice became a trifle emotional. 'He told me it had cost him quite a bit but he wears it always, even in bed, on his wrist, you know that, girl.'

'My God. It couldn't be the same one,' she said.

'Well Eileen, there is only one. It was a private job done with a guarantee that no more would be made like it, and his three brothers' names are on the casing inside.'

'Where is this mate of yours? Where does he work?' Eileen asked.

'He's in the Home Guard, like me. In daytime he does odd jobs for people because he is a little disabled. He suffers from a stomach ulcer. He's probably out tonight, on patrol. Eric Small's his name.'

They had reached her house and Eileen felt the first pangs of fear creep over her as she got out her door key.

'I shall have to go to the hospital. In a couple of hour's time,' Bill said. 'I hope you don't mind. I've got to check.'

She had turned round and had thought he had gone. He had turned his torch out and she had a job to find the key hole to open her door.

'No, it's alright,' she whispered. 'Ask for Matron. Good night and thanks for walking me home.'

'It's good morning,' he answered and then was gone.

Eileen opened her front door as quietly as she could. The black-out regulations prevented her from putting on any lights in the passage so she pulled off her scarf and thick coat and flung it on a chair in the kitchen. Then she crept upstairs to her bedroom, undressed in the dark and slid into bed, afraid of waking Ann up in the next room. It was half past five n the morning but she would get a few hours sleep. She wasn't on duty until the second shift at the hospital which was from two until six. The sheets were as cold as ice but Eileen never had time to think about it. Sleep came swiftly and her dreams were of Jim Blake.

Chapter 3

Ann got up at her usual time and had her breakfast porridge then got ready for work at the factory. She lit the stove as the house was so very cold. 'To hell with the coal,' she thought. She was sure that they would get some more for Christmas, after all, it was three weeks away.

Her sister's coat and scarf lay on the chair and her keys were still on the table. Her time must have been later than she thought as her tea was still in the oven. Now cold, the whale steak had gone a funny colour. She lifted out the plate and emptied the contents into the dustbin just outside of the kitchen door. She began to wish that she had got up at six when she had awoken. Seeing the film of ice on the inside of the window she had returned to the warmth of the bed for another hour. It was then that she had heard the faint movement of Eileen turning in bed and she felt happy now that she knew she was there. They were very close for sisters and the fact that they were twins made the bond even closer. Ann had lain there with her face down deep in the blankets. She had not been able to get back to sleep but had kept wondering why her sister had not come home at her usual time. It was seldom that the nursing staff had such long shifts. It was usually an accident or another emergency at the hospital.

'Poor girl must have been tired out,' she thought and decided to leave her in bed to make up for her loss of sleep.

She banked up the fire and put the old black kettle on the top before she left for work. Her sister would have a nice warm room to come down to later. There was not a sound from upstairs so she must still be asleep.

Ann was back home again half an hour later. She hadn't expected the events which had unfolded on her arrival at the factory: The girls and women had been hanging about outside the factory entrance. It was only the rather old and shabby little school which they worked in but they turned out panels of silk to make parachutes. They didn't work long hours and though she disliked it, the women were nice and friendly. It was a job, after all.

They greeted her as she joined them. 'What are we waiting for?' she asked.

'Well, for a start, we can't get in,' one girl said, crossly. 'Someone saw the men taking all the machines away last night about an hour after we all left. I'll bet you that's it! Our jobs are gone. Without those industrial sewing machines we ain't got jobs.'

'That's right.' A voice came from behind the women and a tall, thick-set man appeared. He was no spring chicken and his voice was sharp. He was a stranger, not the usual boss.

He opened the factory door and motioned them inside. The place was bare. 'There you are. Take your aprons and anything that belongs to you then go!' He handed a small envelope to each one, saying, 'That's your wages up to date.' Some of the girls went straight away. The women took their aprons from the coat pegs and gradually filtered out.

'Down to the Labour Office,' said one girl. 'Got to do war work of some kind. Wonder where they'll send me?'

Ann said goodbye to them and made her way slowly home. It was almost daylight, nearly half-past eight. She hated these dark mornings. As she walked home she bumped into her mum's old friend Mrs Clark, Bill's wife. She was probably on her way to work, Ann thought. She was a cleaner for the big office block down Below Bar. Her and Bill were a nice couple.

'Hello Ann. Fancy seeing you! How's your sister?'

'She's still asleep. Actually she worked all last night as well as her afternoon one. I really don't know what time she came home. I only know that I cooked her tea, put it on a plate in the warm oven and it was still there this morning when I lit the kitchen range. She was too tired to eat it I reckon.'

'Are you not going to work today?' Ethel Clark asked. Ann told her the news about the factory shut down and her worry about getting another job here in Southampton. She so hoped that they would not send her away on war work. She and Eileen didn't want to be separated.

'By the way, that little grocers shop in East Street was ransacked last night, they say. They took sugar, bacon, eggs and other breakfast stuff. They broke in the back way and got away through the Park, so I was told.'

'My God! That's people's rations gone.' Ann frowned.

'Don't want to think about it,' said Ethel. 'Bill hasn't signed off yet. Home Guard may be helping the police. They often co-operate. Must go Ann. Bill will be waiting for his breakfast if he's home. He'll be hungry after all-night duty. I never wanted him to join the Home Guard. He could have helped the war effort some other way.' She looked at Ann and shook her head.

Ann smiled but didn't make any answer. She knew they liked playing soldiers, out every night most of the time propping up the bar in some local pub. All this while their women sat all the evening knitting socks for them and making the rationed food stretch from one to three, after queuing for it for hours. When they felt like listening to the wireless, it was always then that the battery was running low or the accumulator needed re-charging. Ann had heard it all before.

It was only a fifteen minute walk home but it was cold to stand and talk for so long. The wind was bitterly cold and it was still freezing. She put her latch-key in the door and met the sudden warmth in the house. In the kitchen the range glowed red and the kettle on top was boiling. It was heaven, Ann thought as she took off her coat, scarf and the bright woollen gloves that her mother had knitted. She held them for a brief second against her cheek. 'Dear Mum. How I wish you were here!'

There was not a sound. Eileen was still in bed. Ann decided to leave her there. It must have been a rough night in the hospital, she thought. Her sister rarely stopped in bed, always up at six every morning. She glanced at Eileen's time-sheet on the sideboard. With a sigh of relief she saw that Eileen was on two to six today in the Male Ward.

Ann made a pot of tea, and then, drawing up a chair, sat contemplating her loss of work. It was the money she was most concerned about. It would mean signing on the dole.

The employment exchange was a place of fear. You not only had to take the work they offered you, but the fear lay in how far away it would be. If you didn't take the job offered, then you no longer had a choice. They would send you out on war work.

She shuddered as she emptied her pay packet. Fifteen shillings would not get far now Mum was gone. They had to run the house, her and Eileen. Bills, bills. Good thing they didn't have any rent to pay. Coal, gas, electric, insurance. Ann's thoughts were still running around in her head when there was a tap on the back door. She went to see who it was and found Mrs Sharpe standing on the doorstep.

'Come in Emily.'

'Thought I would let you know all the goings-on!' Emily said in a voice subdued in excitement.

'George came home about four o'clock this morning. I heard him come up the stairs and so I quickly put a dressing gown on and faced him.

'"I hope you're not going to start this lark, getting boozed up and coming home all hours!" I said to him. He was so angry with me for saying that. He said 'Shut up! I'll tell you in the morning."

I said. "No George Sharpe you'll explain now." So I put the landing light on and pushed him down the stairs to the kitchen, and followed him. We sat there with cups of tea until five o'clock. He said the men were restless and had gathered in one of the big sheds. Apparently a man in a smart grey suit had informed one of them to gather the workers to this shed and wait for the speaker to come. There was to be a meeting before they left work. It was filling up when George went in with his mate Len. There was about fifty of them there.'

'What was the meeting about?' asked Ann.

'Well, you see . . . That's it! There was no official meeting. The men all waited and then, my God Ann, they suddenly realised it was a hoax, but a bad one because they discovered that they were all locked in. No one had noticed the last man in was distributing cigarettes he had been given. The men were noisy and didn't hear the lock being put on the door. George said there were no windows, only small ventilators because of the blackout. They were locked in all night until four o'clock. You know what? They would probably have been there until 8 o'clock if it had not been for the air raid siren sounding off. All for one German plane, George said. So of course the Air Raid Wardens were crawling all over the docks and when they got close to the shed they heard noises from inside the shed. My! Were they thankful to be let out? They were so angry. If you had appeared at that moment in a grey suit . . . you would have been beaten up and thrown in the sea.'

'What happened afterwards?' said Ann.

'They all dispersed and went home. George said he got hold of an Air Raid Warden and he told my son that it was the work of a fifth columnist. He said, that night, when all was silent, a ship came in. We know that. There was no cargo and it could have been a cargo of men, Germans. They could have slipped in and away, no one about to question them. The police are on their way. They wanted to ask questions of the men. However, they have all gone home.'

'Oh dear, do you think this is getting serious?' asked Ann.

Mrs Sharpe had got up from her chair, but she sat down again and with a worried frown on her face said, 'Do you know what my George told me? Mind you he did say he was advised not to spread it around. But, as it's you Ann, I know it's all right to tell you: He told me the Germans are filtering in to this port in no small way. His policeman friend told him, the chain of Butchers Mottoms, well, they've all got new managers. Ours in East Street and the Fifty Shilling Tailors, all got new people in there. Mind you after bombing the town to bits there are very few shops left here. The ones in what was the cigarette factory in Shirley now making small parts for Spitfires, well, all the workers have been sent to another place and they say it's all new workers in the factory, making army cars. Strange. That big block of offices near the Bargate. It is empty. The people have all gone. George said his mate told him. It appears that his wife used to clean half those offices, her and a younger woman. They had from six in the morning until eight-thirty to clean, five days a week. They have had notice to finish. Awful, isn't it, Ann? Strange things going on.'

Mrs Sharpe got up again and made for the door, saying, 'I must get back, I've said too much now. George warned me to keep my trap shut.'

Ann was left on her own in her kitchen, thinking. It was so quiet. It was a dead town. Few shops. No children.

Chapter 4

Jim Blake woke up with a start. His mother was standing with her head round his bedroom door. 'Jim. You said last night to give you a call about six. You going back to work then?'

'Yes Mother.' He shot out of bed and she shut the door with a sharp snap.

Washed, shaved and dressed, he went downstairs to the kitchen where she had made him a large mug of tea, and had cut him a pile of sandwiches for him to take with him.

'How's your leg?' she asked with a look of worry settling across her face. She was not pleased that he had made up his mind to go back to work. But then she sighed. They had this discussion only last night. 'It's too soon,' she had said, but he was stubborn like his mother, and had won the battle of wills. But he knew deep down that it was a bit soon. The heat from the furnace would probably cause it to itch.

It was Eileen he was thinking about. He needed to be active again and ask her again to go out with him. He was a little unsure, and had no confidence in himself. He had looked at himself grimly in the shaving mirror. What could she see in him?

His mother was filling up a large thermos flask for him. She gave him a smile. 'There's no sugar, son. We have used up our ration until the weekend.'

He screwed up his face, and said, 'Lord, I hate it without sugar. Never mind, I will get round the girl in the canteen at Waterloo Station, she will give me a bit in the flask'.

'You will! You can charm the hairs off a donkey, you can.' His mother gave him the lunch box and he went out into the fresh early morning air of the Forest. It was dark and there were no lights in the sky, even the moon was not out. But Jim knew the Forest like the back of his hand. So he hurried to get the milk train, this would take him right to Southampton Central, where his locomotive would be in the shed waiting for him. His fireman would be there to stoke the fire up and heat the boiler. It would be off to London by eight o'clock sharp.

He reached the local train station where his mate the driver was waiting for him. He hopped on to the footplate and was away. He only did this route in the winter months. Summer time in the New Forest was too nice to ignore. He would get his bicycle out of the shed and mother would say the same thing she always said as he cycled off to Southampton. 'Be careful, Jim. Cheerio.'

He loved that early morning ride. The Forest was beautiful even in the rain. Bob his fireman was there when he arrived. He had lit the fire, filled the water tank, shunted the big engine out of the siding and had two tin mugs of hot cocoa at the ready.

London was quiet. The people still came to sleep on the benches and in the doorways, even on the station. The majority went to the underground tubes to sleep. It was safer than their homes. Tea and coffee was available at the station canteen.

Jim waited until the counter was clear, and he asked the girl if he could have a bit of sugar in his flask. It was the usual girl who he sometimes asked. She gave Jim her special Hollywood smile and touched his hand when he had his flask back. She knew exactly how much he liked in the tea. But this time she slipped a brown bag along by the flask.

'There you are, sir, sandwiches wrapped to take away. Sixpence please, sir.' She was aware of the crowd now coming for tea. Jim put the sixpence coin in her dainty little hand and winked his eye.

'See you, Miss.'

He took it back to the engine. Bob was eating his sandwich, with a grin on his face.

'Naughty!' he said to Jim. 'She's probably married with five kids. But I needed that sugar.' He opened the brown paper bag. 'Bit extra today. Must be her birthday or something.'

'I would get her some chocolate, Bob, but the trouble is she will take it as a sign to take her out, and I've got someone special.'

'Cor lummey! You are a deep one. I've never seen you with a girl'

'Well, I've never bothered with girls,' said Jim. 'At least not since I was seventeen, and found Southampton girls were not like the country ones, they moved too fast for me. This girl is a hospital nurse. It was her who attended to my burns. I got to see her a lot. But being a bit shy I've only just got round to asking her out.'

'Did she say yes?'

'You bet she did, Bob. I'm going to see her later.'

It turned out to be a long day for Jim and Bob. They had not expected the change of timetables, or the fact that one driver had not turned up for a Brighton run. He and his family had been killed by an unexploded bomb in their garden at least a week ago. There had been no one to inform the station. The men were shocked at the news, especially as London had not had a raid for five days. The peaceful nights were riddled with uncertainty.

Jim should have been home by four o'clock. As it was he and Bob got back to Southampton West at six o'clock. His thoughts had been on Eileen all day. He was beginning to wonder how on earth he could have a love life in this job. He took off his boiler suit and washed up in the station toilet. He had decided to find Eileen. If he stopped to go home first and change the time would be running on.

He felt a little awkward and foolish when he arrived at the hospital only to be told by Sister that she had gone off duty only about fifteen minutes ago. He asked for her home address but she declined.

Disappointed and quite a few hours without food, he made his way down the corridor to leave. Matron was walking towards him and she immediately recognised him. Jim stopped and Matron asked after his leg burns, concern in her voice.

He told her how clean it was and healed completely. Then he explained why he was in the hospital. She put him at ease and took him to her office.

Giving him Eileen's address, she asked, 'You are not a married man?' Her sudden question shook his confidence.

'No Ma'am,' he said. 'No commitments.'

'Right then, Mr Blake, here is what you are looking for,' and she handed him a slip of paper with Eileen's address on.

How on earth he got to find number7, Glenmore Road, he never knew. It was pitch black out and he only had a tiny torch. He had left the large one at the station but after one or two blunders he finally found number 7.

Ann answered the door, first speaking through the letter box and asking who it was. She asked him to wait a second while she asked Eileen. Her sister was up from the table like a shot from a cannon.

'Of course I know a Jim Blake,' she shouted at Ann. She put the hall light on and opened the front door quickly.

'Come in quickly,' she said, 'mustn't show a light.'

Jim followed her inside to the warm kitchen. The stove was glowing red and the smell of food made him draw his breath. Ann stirred the large saucepan after a brief greeting. Eileen pulled him towards a chair, and they sat down close to each other. He stared at the white table cloth a bit shyly and didn't know how to start the conversation.

Eileen broke the silence, the nurse side coming to the fore. 'How's the leg?'

He seemed to suddenly find his voice. 'It's fine, thanks. I started back to work today. Actually I've not been home yet, so excuse the work clothes.'

'What difference do they make? Have you eaten?'

'Yes!' He hesitated for a second. 'Well, I had a sandwich at two-o'clock at Waterloo Station.'

She smiled at him and their eyes met as she said, 'Well, Jim Blake, why don't you join us? Do you like rabbit stew? 'Cos that's what we got.'

'Yes! Please.'

The warmth in her voice and the fact that she had slid her hand in his surprised him. He would have eaten a bowl of turnips just to sit at table with her by his side. Ann put a brimming hot plate of stew in front of him. She looked straight at him for the first time.

'My God! You two are alike,' he muttered, looking first at one girl and then the other. The sisters both laughed at the same time.

'Well, Jim, we are twins. Identical twins at that.' Eileen passed him a spoon as well as a knife and fork, and with her other hand she squeezed his.

When she took their empty plates away, Ann found herself studying him. His lovely blue eyes shaded by black lashes. His dark hair that was thick and crispy. Nice hands for a man. She felt a pang of envy pass over her. Why did Eileen always get the cream?

She left them to talk while she washed the dishes. Then on a sudden impulse and a little white lie, she said, 'I'm sorry I have to go, Eileen. Mrs Sharpe asked me to go round her place and help her with something.'

Eileen looked puzzled. 'What something?'

'I think it's aprons, she cut them, but can't sew. She wants me to machine them up for her.'

'That's what you get for sewing parachutes at work. She thinks you of all people can sew,' said Eileen with a laugh.

But her laugh was warm, contented, with the tiniest spark of excitement in it. It meant that she could be alone with Jim, if only for an hour. Their eyes met as the back door shut with a click and her sister's footsteps sounded on the backyard stone floor. They heard Mrs Sharpe's high pitch voice say, 'Do come in, Ann.'

Dr John Shaw made his way to the Men's Ward. Matron had been to see him and discuss the matter of the three fishermen. He was now going to discharge them. She had told him to make sure they were quite fit to leave and she suggested he tell them to go to the Seamen's Mission below Bargate. They would see that all the men got back to their homes. They would also know all there was to know about their capsized fishing trawler.

John entered the Men's Ward and was surprised to see the empty beds. The fishermen had gone! Dr Preston had given them their clothes back and had sent them along to the patients' waiting room to wait for Dr Shaw, to sign them off. Exasperated at all the fuss bestowed on these men, John Shaw made his way to the waiting room.

Once again his temper grew where he found it empty. They had really gone this time.

His next move was to find Matron. He was about to knock the door of her office when he heard voices inside, it sounded like authority too. He took a chance and tapped the door.

'Come in,' said a very flustered Matron.

There were two police officers with her and two detectives in plain clothes. The subject they were discussing was none other than three fishermen. Matron was angry and still on the defence.

'Of course they were genuine,' she insisted. 'Were you here? No!'

She told them that they spoke well and knew the coastline; they even knew a little village in Kent where Matron had lived. Even the name of the pub, 'The Sailor's Hat'.

'Of course they weren't Germans,' she snapped. She sent for the ward sister, but she knew little as she had not come on duty until eight that morning. She had been off sick with a mild flu bug. But she said the captain was a nice man. He showed her the names of his three children inside of his watch. George, Fred and William, who was five, he had told her.

The police left Matron's office and spoke to a couple of nurses before they left the hospital. They asked for a Nurse Smith, but Dr Shaw said it was not her turn; she would be on at two till six and in the Women's Ward.

Mrs Small came slowly into the hospital. It was just as the police were coming out. It sent shivers down her spine, seeing them.

'It must be Eric. An accident? Ah! That was it!' she half muttered to herself. 'He must have had an accident. It wasn't safe going out every night with guns.' A picture formed in her mind of her husband coming in this entrance on a stretcher. Eric was injured, that was it. Her Eric was probably asking for her.

A nurse approached her and asked if she could help. Poor soul looked lost, she thought, giving her a smile.

Mrs Small tried to explain, but the nurse sent her to the receptionist at the desk nearby.

'No! There is no one of that name admitted within the last twenty-four hours.' The lady was kind but firm.

'Why did you think the worst, Mrs Small? He may have worked overtime,' she suggested, 'or gone for a pint.'

'No, he always had the same hours,' she said, nearly in tears.

'What does he do?' The receptionist was getting as confused as her.

'Oh! He's on war work. Eric is in the Home Guard.'

'Ah! I see!' The revelation was all she needed, and taking Mrs Small's hand with an air of importance, she said, 'Ah! A man of authority. And protecting us, too. You must be proud of him. Now you go home and wait. He will turn up, you'll see.'

She gave Daisy Small another friendly pat and turned away, watching as the little lady in her fur hat and brown winter coat walked slowly out of the big doors, her mission not accomplished.

Eric Small had been on duty all night. But then that was the night before. He should have come home in the morning but he hadn't and then not last night. It was too long. Daisy was confused, so much so, that she had not been to bed. She had slept in the chair waiting for him.

The Company Captain had missed him on parade. He became anxious and went to the house. It was one of a terrace of cottages and he rapped on the door.

Daisy was home, but very tired. She had searched, going in all the pubs and even the bookies. But no one had seen Eric since his night duty when he and another man had pulled the fishermen on to the shore. She explained his disappearance to the Captain who later mustered up the men and formed a Home Guard search party.

One of the group who was most affected was Eric's mate Bill Clarke. He was worried about the watch. He dare not say anything yet! It was too early. Find Eric first. Alive!

Bill joined the search party. The protective barbed wire had been cut in three places. No easy task as whoever cut it must have had strong wire cutters and why were they not seen?

The searchers agreed, it had been very dark moonless skies for several nights. The Home Guard and the Air Raid wardens all agreed you just couldn't see your own hand in front of you.

'Let's see if they left any clues,' Bill said, as he walked to where a tiny shed stood silent, age worn.

The Home Guard used this for shelter in really bad weather. It was useful and you could see ships coming into the docks with just a good pair of binoculars.

One of the men wrestled with the lock on the door. He thought it strange because it was never locked. It took three of them to eventually get the shabby wooden door open.

The sight that met their eyes was something they would never forget. No one made a sound. They stood like cold stone statues and stared in horror at the body of Eric Small, Home Guard, curled up dead on the floor. He had been shot. His helmet, still covered with army disguise net, lay on the floor beside him but his rifle was missing. Perhaps they had shot him with his own gun.

Bill Clarke was the first to speak. 'See if his watch ...' He went to move the cuff on Eric's uniform and felt the Captain's hand on his arm.

'Stop, Clarke!' he said brusquely. 'Don't touch! Don't anyone touch! Do you hear? We have to get the police. This is out of our hands. It is a police matter. I will leave you two here to stand guard while we go to the police station right away. Don't let anyone come any closer than this!'

He took a step back and scuffed the ground with his foot. The two men nodded and took up their positions.

Bill Clarke felt sick inside. 'Who would do this?' he thought. But still the thing that roused his anger was the watch. He would know if Eric still had it on his wrist, as soon as the Police came to move the body. 'If he doesn't have the watch on, and it isn't anywhere in the hut, then God help that fisherman,' he thought. 'I'll tell the police. My God I will.'

It was over half an hour before the police arrived. They took away the body of Eric Small and not before Bill Clarke had asked them to look for his watch. It was not on Eric's wrist, or in any of his pockets. The men searched the floor of the hut and ground around it. There was nowhere complicated to look. The surrounding shore line was out of bounds apart from the places where the barbed wire had been cut. It was bleak, nothing but concrete blocks. The police started to become a little frosty with Bill, suggesting that this must be a very valuable watch.

He took their jibes and the two men themselves were then searched. But still no watch. Bill kept quiet about the sentimental value of it. He just told them that Eric was wearing it when he and Bill started their patrol night duty, and it was special to him, not money value.

The police sent them home and Bill was not sorry. Two policemen stayed on the spot to guard the hut until the fingerprint men came.

Bill's thoughts were with Daisy, Eric's wife. He decided to go and see her and took his wife Ethel with him. It was a good move because the two women fell into each other's arms. He was useful, as he carried her suitcase when she left to go and stay with them for a few days.

They had no children so Daisy was on her own. She needed Bill and Ethel for a while. He had been Eric's best mate for many years; in the Home Guard together from the first day. He felt very sad now.

Two plain clothed policemen came to see Bill Clarke that evening. He took them into the sitting room, which was only used on Sundays or special occasions. The two women stayed in the kitchen. After being questioned about his friendship with the dead man he decided to tell them the whole story of the wrist watch. They then asked Bill who he thought might have envied it, and been tempted into taking it.

He told them no one knew about the face on the watch. Eric was sentimental about it, and it was his secret. He hesitated about telling the police that Nurse Smith had seen it under one of the fishermen's pillows that night. The trouble was, had she really seen the real one. There were hundreds manufactured, as it was a new trend in place of the old-fashioned pocket watches. The watch she saw sounded exactly like it, but he was reluctant to get her involved.

He need not have worried, because the next question was about the fishermen. The police needed to know the name of the Doctor who treated them, and who dragged the men from the sea.

Bill suggested that they should go to the hospital and ask for Dr Preston, the House Doctor, also nurse Eileen Smith who attended to the men.

The policemen shook Bill's hand and thanked him for his help. 'Keep the whole thing quiet,' they asked. 'We don't want to scare people. We'll interview Mrs Small later.'

As they were about to leave, one of the men said in a quiet voice, 'The Special Branch are on the look out. We've had hundreds of German spies slip into this country since the end of November. It's bad.'

After they left, Bill went back to the warm kitchen where the two women were laying the table for supper.

'Damn cold in the other room', he said.

'What did they want?' asked Ethel.

'Nothing much,' he said lightly. 'Mostly about the Home Guard. It is very seldom you get an accident.' The last sentence was for the benefit of Daisy. It was too soon for the truth, and tears were running down her thin pale cheeks.

Ethel put an arm round her. That was just like her. Wonderful friend with so much love to give away, he thought. His Ethel was everything to him. He went across and put his arm round the two of them.

Eileen finished cleaning the bedrooms and Ann said that she would do the downstairs. They had both finished and Eileen made a few slices of toast between them. They usually made sandwiches at lunch time, but there was nothing to put in them. One look in the larder had revealed no cheese, no spam, and no tinned fish. So they had settled for toast. At least there was a bowl of beef dripping, but even that had shrunk to about an inch thick layer. There was bread anyway!

They sat at the kitchen table and discussed the shopping. The grocery stores they went to were almost empty as robbers had more or less cleaned them out.

'How about Liptons? Was that bombed?' Ann went on chewing a burnt crust of bread.

'No! Try there! See what they have for our ration coupons. You want me to go?' asked Ann.

'Well, you do have the time now you are finished at the factory. I have my job at the hospital.'

'You could have done it this morning,' muttered Ann.

'Yes! But wait a minute; I couldn't leave you all the cleaning. We usually share the jobs.'

'All right, I'll go. I still have to call in and sign off at the Labour Exchange,' said Ann, brightening up.

'Well, we at least got our tea tonight. There's plenty of soup and vegetables left in that pot, even if there is no rabbit.'

Eileen smiled. 'Yes!' she answered dreamily. 'It was lovely sharing it with Jim Blake last night.'

'You seeing each other again?' asked Ann, enviously.

'Yes! He's taking me to meet his mother tomorrow. I'm on Clinic duty only. So I shall be home at twelve noon. We are going on the bus to Cadnam, and then it's only ten minutes' walk to Beech Cottage.'

'Well I think you'd better be off to work. Look at the time. You're on at two o'clock aren't you?'

'Yes!' Eileen pulled her coat on quickly and looked for her scarf.

Ann was washing up the cups and plates out in the scullery when she heard the front door snap, and her sister's, 'Bye Sis' as it did.

Chapter 5

Eileen was five minutes late at the hospital. Matron was there and frowned. 'I like my nurses to be right on time Nurse Smith,' she snapped. 'There are two detectives in my office waiting about to interview you.'

The plain clothed officer told her to sit down while they asked her some questions. Eileen knew it would be about the fishermen, and she was right. But their next ones were about the watch. There was no other way but to tell them. All the same, she was surprised.

'Did you learn all about the watch from Bill Clarke? You thought it was just an ordinary wrist watch, and you had not noticed it was different.'

'No! I had caught a glimpse of something metallic under one of the fishermen's pillows. I took it out and looked at it for quite a few minutes.' Nurse Smith could see that Matron was cross.

'Yes! Go on please.' The policeman gave Eileen a friendly smile.

'Well, Sir, it was ten minutes slow, so I turned the little hands and set it at the right time for him.'

'Was that it?' Matron tried to interrupt but he stopped her.

'No, Sir, I noticed one of the figures, eleven, was different to the other numerals. It had a tiny cross in place of the eleven, and there were three gold dots, very minute on the cross. I was lucky to see it. You could miss it if the hand was on eleven o'clock. It was so unusual. The back opened and three names were inscribed on the metal. It was George, Fred and William. I do remember that.'

'Who were these three people?' asked one of the men.

'They were Eric's three older brothers, all killed in the First World War. That's why there were three golden dots on the tiny cross. But I only knew about the dots and the names when I told Mr Clarke. He walked me home from the hospital the night before last. I told him about the watch and he simply said that I had discovered Eric's secret, if it was his watch.'

'And is it, do you think nurse?'

'Well it's got to be, Sir, because Eric had that face specially made with the cross and eleven for Armistice Day Remembrance. Why don't you ask Mr Small? He would show you, if he has his.'

The two men had listened carefully, not revealing Eric's death.

'Is that what you think nurse?'

'Oh yes. There is not another watch in the world the same. The jeweller signed a form to pledge he would never make a copy.'

'Really! Well thank you Nurse Smith for all your help. Can we see the watch? This other man's watch?'

'No, he took it with him,' she replied. 'I couldn't stop him. In fact, he said the names of his children were inscribed in the back. His three sons. I had nothing to go on, as I had never seen it before. I came off duty after doing the night shift. When I came in yesterday they had all gone. I wish I had known about it before. I just thought it was his watch.'

'All right nurse, you can go now,' said Matron. 'Load of rubbish this all is. They were nice men and they had been very sick.'

'Did they speak good English Matron?' asked one of the policemen.

'Yes. They were English – or British,' she sounded offended, as if a Matron of a hospital couldn't tell an Englishman from a German. 'Good gracious me! They were British, they came from Whitby.'

'Right! Thank you Matron. Now we wish to speak to a Doctor Preston if you please.'

Matron rose to her feet and sent her nurse on first. Eileen gave a sigh of relief that it was all over. The one she felt sorry for was kind Doctor Preston. My God, what would he say? She knew he did not think the three men were fishermen. He had said so that night. He had examined their skin and hair and had said that they had not been in the sea for very many minutes. He had reckoned that a boat had brought them in, dropping them near the shore line. But being such a dark night, they had had a little bit further to swim since they had underestimated the nearness of the shore.

Nurse Smith went back to the Women's Ward where she had been transferred to. It seemed a long shift and time dragged. Most of her patients were fresh ones in.

Then the doors opened and in walked Doctor Shaw. Eileen had forgotten about him and he immediately turned on the charm. They had to be careful as Matron did not approve of flirting or dating between the staff. John asked her if she would meet him outside at six thirty when she

57

came off duty, then they could plan some time together. There was only one cinema left after the last bombing raid, but there was a good film on. Eileen shifted from one foot to another as she stood in silence.

'I'm so sorry John. I've got a regular friend now. He is a train driver. We get on well together.' She trailed off, not quite sure what else to say.

'That's all right, Nurse Smith. Thank you for telling me.' His manner and face took on a formal Doctor-Nurse situation. Ward Sister had come in and she could see why he had taken a stiff formal attitude.

'Ah! Doctor Shaw I need to talk to you about a patient.' Sister Jones went across to her desk and he followed.

Eileen looked at her watch and wondered if Jim would come to the house. She longed to see him again. They had planned on going to meet his mother tomorrow, but it was a long time to wait. Tomorrow was almost years away. Her thoughts on Jim Blake sort of petered out and they turned to her sister, Ann. She had seen that tiny glimpse of jealousy when she had first me him. Her eyes had refused to meet Eileen's, but she had made Jim feel so very welcome in their home.

Stupid, she had become emotional and felt like crying for what? For nothing. Sister Jones asked her to put a dressing on the young girl's head. She had just come in after an accident. Masonry had fallen on her in the house. People still lived in partly bombed buildings that looked safe but it was not until a few days had elapsed that the occupants discovered they were not structurally sound. The hospital had taken in many such cases lately.

'Our 'ouse is fallin' down,' the girl had said.

Sister Jones had taken over from her when she saw the depth of the wound. The gash was over four inches in length. The towel holding it together was anything but clean. It had once been white but now was a coffee colour with large grey areas.

'That's our Ma's towel. We want it back,' Eileen heard her say.

The Sister was just about to put it in a waste bin, so she gave the blood-soaked towel to Nurse Smith with a crisp,' Here! Get this laundered for her to take home. I doubt they have any washing facilities.'

How right she was.

She hurried home at six and found her sister Ann silently weeping. Eileen wrapped her arms around her and cried too. 'I knew it,' she said, 'I've been crying for the least little thing at work.'

'For God's sake, Ann, what are we crying for?' She released her hold and went to the dresser for cups.

'We'll have a cup of tea, we'll feel better then!'

'I've been to the Labour Exchange,' said Ann sharply.

'Right! Well, let's hear the good news or the bad, shall we?'

Eileen busied herself with making the tea. She didn't want to look at Ann's face. She was the older sister by five minutes, so she had to look after Ann, her younger sister. It was funny; she always had to, even when they were small children.

'Well! I suppose it's not all that bad. I shall still be sleeping at home. But it will be a long day. You will have to do the shopping now ...' she trailed on.

'Well, come on Ann, tell us where it is. I take it you got a job. But doing what?'

'It's a nursery. No, not children, it's flowers and tomatoes.'

'Where, for Heaven's sake?'

'It's a village in the New Forest. The man said I shall know when I get there. There are no road signs anywhere now. Well, you know that.'

'What do you have to do?' Eileen looked sceptically at her sister. 'You? You can't grow a runner bean in the garden. It runs away.'

'Well I have to do my job whatever it is.'

'How are you getting there? Bus? It will cost you half your wages travelling there and back each day.'

Ann shook her head. 'Oh no, it won't be bus. They have a little van and he said something about pick-up places. They pick up the women near the Bargate, so I suppose I have to wait there.'

'What time?' asked Eileen.

'Eight o'clock in the winter, and seven in the summer. So the man said.'

'He seems to say a lot, this man! Didn't you have to go for an interview?' Eileen pushed the tea in front of her as she said it. She didn't like the sound of this job; it resulted in spilling her tea.

'No! It is war work. Classed as Land Army. They can send you anywhere now. The man said you have to go.'

'Well I guess we are making a fuss. It could have been worse, Ann. In fact, I'll help you. Our Mum had a big book on gardening, nursery work and how to grow tomatoes. I will find it. I'm sure it will help.'

'Thanks,' Ann said, looking at the cup of tea, with tea in the saucer, tea on the table top. 'You are good at this.' She grinned at Eileen and winked her eye.

'You really should get a job in the Canteen. Serving tea. You don't have an interview for that either.'

Jim Blake had mixed feelings about the evening. He longed to see Eileen, but he was a little unsure of the meeting he was obliged to attend. The meeting was at eight o'clock in the Civic Centre. The whole thing had been sudden and shrouded in mystery.

He had decided to look in to see Eileen first. He hated the thought of being underhand with her, but he was told to keep quiet about the meeting.

Eileen's face lit up like a beacon when she answered his knock on the door. He held her tightly to him in the dim-lit hall, and then she took his hand and led him to the kitchen, where Ann was clearing away their dishes from the evening meal.

'Hello, Jim.' Their eyes met for a brief moment, and then she hurried out to the scullery. Lovely, shy, Ann.

They sat and talked for a few minutes in whispers. Ann rattled the cups and dishes, making noises that were not important. After a while, Jim rose to his feet. 'I must go,' he said.

'But you have been home and changed, and had a shave,' she said, softly drawing her long fingers across his chin. 'Can't you stay?'

'No. I'm sorry. I have to meet a mate, another driver for a drink. Then I have to get home early. I've jobs to do before the morning. You know. I'm away at six.'

She gazed up at him and wrinkled her nose.

'All right. We are seeing each other tomorrow?' Her eyes pleaded with him not to say no.

'Yes of course. I finish at twelve midday tomorrow. You too. Mum is expecting us.'

He suddenly remembered the rabbit in his overcoat pocket. Throwing it on the kitchen table with a grin, he said, 'There's a dinner for you.'

'That is wonderful. We can eat now!' The thought of eating it was slightly spoiled by the glassy eyes, staring at her. She stroked its fur with one finger.

'Come and look Ann,' she shouted.

Jim buttoned up his coat. 'I'll see myself out,' he said bending over her. His lips brushed hers, and then he was gone.

'Who's going to skin this and cut it up?' asked Eileen. The two girls stood staring at the rabbit.

'Dunno!'

'The ones from the Butcher are all cut up ready. Mum knew how to do this sort of thing. I know! Let's ask Ethel next door.'

Chapter 6

Jim Blake let himself into the cottage. It was all quiet. His Mum had gone to bed; this was her usual time, ten o'clock. She was always up early in the morning, six o'clock. The cottage was small but warm. They had plenty of wood to keep two fires going, but the kitchen was warm still from her cooking. On the table covered in a white tea-cloth, was a freshly baked cake. He smiled to himself. She was doing this baking for Eileen.

The bedroom was fresh but not cold. The thatched roof helped that, he decided. He was a long time going to sleep, though. It had been a strange meeting: Jim had been ushered into a small room where four detectives in plain clothes were waiting for him. In the middle of the room, sitting stiffly at the large oak desk was a high-ranking Army officer. After a moment's rather awkward silence, the four men showed their credentials and as they were about to explain the purpose of the meeting, there was a tap at the door and yet another man entered the room, with apologies for being late.

Jim felt his heart miss a beat. What in God's name was he doing here. He looked at the short stocky figure in a black overcoat. It was the Station Master. Mr Wallace had been Station Master for over twenty years and Jim had always got on well with him, though he didn't see a lot of him.

'You two already know each other I believe,' said one of the men. He didn't wait for Jim to answer, but went on to explain their reason for being there tonight.

The two railway men were asked to take part in a watch and spy campaign. They asked Jim to stand on the footplate and see who got off the train at Waterloo Station, also who got on. The Station Master was asked to pick out the regulars who went to and fro to London, but most of all the strangers, the odd ones who seemed to stand out among the crowds.

Jim was asked if he was willing to do this for his country. He agreed and quite willingly signed a Secrets Act document. Mr Wallace did likewise.

They were given a small pin brooch with R.W. on it. The officer sitting at the desk explained these. He said, 'Wear it and when asked you say 'Railway Worker.' Now the correct title is Rail Workers. There will be a few people with these. They are doing the same surveillance activities. Now listen closely. If someone says 'Railway Workers', then they are frauds, not to be trusted. If they say 'Rail Worker', they are genuine. You must look out for these men. You can help each other with what will often be vital information. Do you understand?'

'Yes, Sir. I'll look out and do my best,' said Jim.

'It must be discreet. Don't draw attention to yourself.' The man at the desk spoke firmly, but put out his hand and shook the men by the hand. It was a sign that the meeting was over.

Mr Wallace went back to his home in Totton and Jim hurried back to the bus that ran two and fro in the Forest. He would have liked to have had a beer with Sid Wallace, but if he did he would miss the last bus to Calmore.

He turned in his bed and tried to wipe out the evening. It was difficult. For one thing he knew he must never tell Eileen. This was something he would have to be careful about, and keep it from her. He was thinking how much he disliked deceiving her, when sleep overtook him.

Eileen was first up and away in the morning. It was still dark at six-thirty. She gave Ann a cup of tea in bed as a treat before she left. Ann did not start work until eight o'clock. It was her first day. Eileen wished her good luck as she left.

Ann cut herself some sandwiches and after having a bowl of porridge she grabbed her coat and let herself out of No. 7. There were two women waiting at the Bargate. Come to think of it, she had seen them before somewhere. She managed a weak smile and approached them.

'Are you both waiting for Dobbs' van, the Wick Lane Nurseries?' she asked.

'Yes.' They flashed her a warm smile. One put her hand out as she spoke. 'We've been there two years. My name's Ivy – Mrs Saunders.' She was the taller of the two and slim, quite well dressed and Eileen was taken aback to see such beautiful hands. She wondered what on earth she was doing at a nursery. Those hands had never done rough work, certainly not gardening, she thought.

'And I'm Mrs Bailey – Gwen.'

As the shabby little van approached them and stopped, Mrs Bailey stood to one side and let Ann get in first. Gwen was plump and in her fifties. Her pink round face was a background for mirth. Within a few seconds she was laughing as her fat bottom pushed into Ann on the wooden seat in the back of the van. There were two hessian sacks placed for them to sit on.

'Be careful of the upholstery,' she joked, in between laughs.

'Oooh! It's posh, I didn't expect such luxury,' said Ann giggling

'High quality from Tyrell and Green,' Gwen continued.

'My name's Ann Smith, by the way,' interrupted Ann.

'Ah! Another boaster with the rare name of Smith,' Gwen laughed again and nudged Ann's shoulder. 'I like you. You'll do. Welcome aboard Ann. I hope you stay. Most of our girls left last year to go in the Forces. You aren't likely to do that are you?'

'No, I live with my twin sister in our parents' old house. She's a hospital nurse.' There was pride in the way she said it.

'Where's the other lady?' Ann asked.

'Oh, my dear, she sits up with the driver.' Gwen's face changed. 'She works in the office, but then she went to a better school than me. My Ma had nine kids and I never went to school very often.'

Ann didn't make any reply, but she smiled warmly and tried to see out of the wide crack in the double door just where they were.

She didn't have to wait many minutes, and the doors were pulled apart and they jumped out of the van into country scenery. Just fields, hedges and trees.

'This is Wick Lane. You can see the glasshouses now from here. Come on, you stay with me, and I will show you where to go, Ann.'

As they walked on Ann passed a large brick house and a barn. Then there was a small wooden shed with a door marked Office Staff Only.

Gwen waited while Ann tapped the office door. A tall broad-shouldered man came out, closing the door quickly. He introduced himself as owner, Manager. He asked for her ID card and asked her a few questions. It was all done so swiftly.

'Go to Number One House and tell Joe I sent you. You will work under him.' He gave her a nod and moved quickly away, leaving her standing there.

'I'm here!' A voice came from behind a small shed nearby and Gwen emerged still with a grin on her face.

'Come with me I'll introduce you to Joe. He's in charge of Number One House. You'll like him, Ann. The only thing is he swears a lot. But he is a kind man.'

Ann followed her and she met Joe, who put her to work straight away. She was given a pair of overalls that were a little too big for her, but she turned up the bottom of the trouser leg and did the same with the sleeves. There were nice big pockets so she stuffed her gloves in them. Looking across at the door where she had just hung her coat up, she realised her mistake in wearing her best coat. She would know better tomorrow. With a shaky hand she took the pile of empty flower pots, which were heavier than expected and looked at the bag of shell he had placed for her to use.

Five minutes later she had come to experience the truth behind Gwen's statement. He certainly swore a lot. It was true. Joe certainly did have a temper and the swearing was like a verse from the Devil in poetry.

His voice rose and fell and with it came his arms and hands. Ann stood stock still, her blood running cold. She had thought for one minute he was about to strike her. Then quite suddenly, like you had turned off a tap inside of him, he stopped. He stood still as a statue.

With a red face he said quietly,' Oh dear! You foolish woman. I did not say fill them to the brim with shell.' He paused for breath, and when he continued his face was flushed and little beads of perspiration ran down his temples and forehead. 'Here! Sit down on this box a minute and I will try and explain it,' he whispered. 'See! All you need is a small handful in the bottom of each one. Then you fill up the rest of the pot with this moist special soil. Not quite to the top.'

Ann stared at the pots and finally found her voice. When it came out it didn't sound like hers. She gulped, 'Sorry! I'm sorry!'

Joe patted her on the shoulder. 'That's all right. Don't be afraid. We all make mistakes,' he said quietly.

Ann glanced at her watch and wondered how she was going to manage another six and a half hours, working here. She longed to turn back the clock and be at the big department store again. Joe had asked her what job she had done before. When she told him, he had grinned at her and said, 'Dear me! You'd better put those gloves on. They're not made just to go into pockets. Get them on!'

From that minute on she sensed his approval. Lunch break came quicker than she expected. She retrieved her sandwiches from her coat pocket and suddenly remembered her flask of tea that she had left on the kitchen table at home. Joe noticed, so he shared his flask of hot strong tea with her, laughing when she said how black it was.

Ann did the return journey in the same way. At four o'clock the two women got in the back of the van but this time it was only her and Gwen. Ivy did not join. She was about to ask the whereabouts of Mrs Saunders, until she read the message in Gwen's eyes.

Gwen Bailey put her fingers to her lips. As soon as the van started moving she whispered, 'Don't ever ask questions here. You'll find out who's taking whose wife out, without losing your innocence. Saves back stabbing.'

Ann nodded her head, but said nothing. All that she thought of was the quickly fading light. It would be dark before she got home. Home would be cold and empty too. Eileen would be out. She was going to meet Jim's mother. Of course they would stay a while, as Eileen was working at the hospital until twelve midday. They would not be back until nine or ten tonight.

When she got home the cold hit Ann as she entered the kitchen. The fire had not been lit, but Eileen had left it laid ready with dry sticks and a small bucket of coal. She put the light on as it was now dark. Curtains were still across from six this morning. She lit the fire in the kitchen range, put the kettle on the top hob and went to the larder to see what she could find to eat. The rabbit still had his fur coat on, but surprise, there were two pork sausages on a plate. The little scrap of paper still clung to the dish. Ann read the words on it.

'I'm sharing my sausages with you girls. I got two for me, two for George, and two for you. Love from Ethel Sharpe.'

Eileen had given her a door key when their mother died. She was trustworthy, a lovely neighbour, and the girls were grateful for her help. It was obvious that she had been in and left the sausages for them today.

'Bless you, Ethel,' murmured Ann. She cooked a large potato, cut it up into slim rounds and fried them. She scraped the bowl using up the rest of the dripping, and then she cooked the sausages. With warm food inside her and warm by the fire, she fell asleep in her Mum's old rocking chair. Twenty years old, thin from lack of food, and months without enough sleep and bombs showering down around them. The last eight days had been unreal, the quiet, and the silent nights. But the habit of listening for those noises in the sky, afraid to sleep, was hard to get rid of. There had been an air of uncertainty for the last few days. People were nervous and Ann, although so young, had been one of them.

Eileen had been obliged to run the clinic on her own. Another nurse had not turned up for work. Doctor Shaw had been there, but the list for injections and dressings had grown from the previous week.

Without a break she had reduced the crowded surgery to the last one, who was a newcomer and who seemed to have no identification on him.

Doctor Shaw had planned to ask Eileen out but it was twelve o'clock and the morning clinic should have finished long before this. It was all going wrong. He frowned as the last one was called and to make things worse, Nurse Smith was anxious for his help. It was serious. Eileen had removed the strips of torn sheeting from the next patient's arm and was shocked to see the wound and amount of blood he had lost. She handed him over to Doctor Shaw.

'Right! You need a few stitches in that arm. How did you do this? It looks very much like a tear from barbed wire. It has to be to tear the flesh like this.' The man seemed reluctant to explain and just nodded his head. 'So it was barbed wire!' Doctor Shaw looked annoyed. 'Then why are you unable to tell me where this happened? They tell me you have no identity card.' Doctor Shaw stopped. He was just in time to catch his patient as he collapsed. Eileen rushed to help and between them, they got him on to a trolley and wheeled him to the accident room. Doctor Shaw asked Eileen to fetch Matron and to make up a bed in the Men's Ward as the patient would need to be watched over that night. Eileen felt disappointed at the turn of events as it meant that she would not get off duty for quite a while but the hospital only kept going because the doctors and nurses pulled together to make it work.

An hour and a half later Eileen managed to come off duty at last. Jim was waiting for her in the entrance hall where he had found a seat. He gave her a big smile as she walked towards him.

It was two o'clock before they arrived at Beech Cottage. Jim pushed open the wicket gate and Eileen gazed at the pretty cottage with her heart in her mouth. It was even nicer inside, as Jim's mother led her towards the open fire and two comfy chairs. 'I'm so happy to meet you. Jim has told me all about you.' She gave Eileen a lovely smile. Her voice was warm and friendly. She was only a little woman, white hair piled high on top of her head, to make her look taller.

Jim had told her that his mum had married late in life, and had him when she was forty. Eileen felt a little bit guilty when she told them both that she had kept the dinner hot. She had expected them about one, so Jim explained to her about hospital work and casualties and Eileen joined in to say how sorry she was. But the atmosphere was so lovely, that it really did not matter.

Afterwards, Eileen said to Jim, that it was the most delicious dinner she had eaten since her own mum had died. 'Roast chicken,' she informed him, 'you only have at Christmas. Please don't let me close my eyes Jim. When I open them it would all disappear, like a dream.'

He took her hand from under the tablecloth and squeezed it. It touched him to the heart. Him, Jim Blake, who took it all for granted. Eggs! Your own chicken, milk from the farm, and rabbits all around, even in the garden. There was always a meal on his table. Suddenly he was seeing life as it was. The empty basket or the full one – it depended on where you live.

As Eileen lay in his arms that night, Jim could feel her ribs. He vowed to look after her. She was everything he wanted in life. In such a short time he loved her, and wanted to spend the rest of his life with her. She was much frailer than he had thought, but he felt sorry for her. A pang of guilt had swept through him as he left her at five o'clock in the morning in her bed.

After he had brought her home the night before, they had been tempted. She had insisted that he stay the night. Making up the bed in the little box room he had agreed. He had known that the buses and trains had gone hours ago.

Ann was in her neighbour's house. Mrs Sharpe had come to take her in to play cards. She had enjoyed the evening and George had been in a pleasant mood, fussing over her, though it was only because he won half a crown, and he promised to treat her to a bar of chocolate, using the sweet coupons from his ration book.

She was late in. The house was quiet and she guessed Eileen had gone up to bed, which she had. What she didn't know was Jim Blake was asleep in the box room, and her sister was lying awake until she heard her come in. Eileen could not sleep but at two o'clock she tiptoed into the little box room being careful not to fall over the boxes, the spare mattress or the little iron bed where Jim lay sleeping. Being so slender she squeezed in bed beside him. The shock made him jump. She put her hand over his mouth and they lay quiet. Jim Blake just held her slim body.

Suddenly a surge of fear took over from the love and longing inside her. She pulled away from Jim, frightened at the risk she had been about to take, so unprepared. The last thing she needed now was a baby. With a soft whimper she slid out of bed and ran back to her own. Tears ran down her cheeks as she pulled the covers up and buried her face in the pillow. Jim meanwhile had not made a sound. He lay there wide awake until the early hours of the morning.

They were having breakfast when she found courage to tell Ann that Jim had slept in the box room because he had missed the train.

'Oh!' Ann looked surprised and gave her sister a look of concern. 'I didn't hear him. No. I didn't even hear him leave. What will the neighbours say?'

'Don't worry about them,' Eileen said. 'He was gone by the time I got up. Anyhow, these dark mornings who is going to see? You can't see your own nose these days since the blackout. I miss the street light in my bedroom, don't you?'

'Just make sure for me, will you Ann. Bang on his door.'

Ann came down laughing. 'Yes, he's gone. Made his own bed too. He can come again. Don't need much looking after.'

Chapter 7

Christmas came round quickly. An empty time, made sad by the shortage of food. Ann had the most time off, but the hospital still had to go on from day to day. However, Eileen did have Christmas day off. The girls did their best to brighten up the sitting room. One evening was spent making paper chains, something they had not done for many years.

Then Eileen Sharpe came in for the evening, bringing her usual bits and pieces to show them. She was very taken by her paper strips. From a packet of red crepe paper, she cuts slices off the folded end into two-inch strips. These stretched in to double the length when unfolded and pulled. The girls looked at each other and tried not to laugh.

'Ah! It's not finished yet,' said Ethel. 'You have to pull one each end and twist. It's the twist that makes it.'

Eileen walked with it to the other side of the kitchen and Ethel held the other end and twisted it. A quite attractive whirl in the paper made a good hanging piece to go with the paper chains.

'The Grocer showed me,' Ethel said. 'He has it down the side of his shop windows. It looked all right too.'

'He couldn't have been very busy to stop and show you this,' Eileen said, as she put the now sadly unfurled paper back on the table

'No! He didn't have much to sell. Most of the shelves were empty but he saved me a bit of bacon and two packets of dried egg powder.'

'Well! I made him some warm woollen socks for nothing.'

'I thought they were for the troops,' Ann muttered.

'Well! It's the same thing; his son is in the Army. He said he would pass them on as soon as this freezing weather eases up. Do you know,' she went on, 'his feet get so cold standing in that shop, and they go blue!'

'Oh Ethel, have you seen them?' Ann started laughing.

'Now you are laughing at me.' She picked up her box of small home-made paper flowers, and made to go, back to her own kitchen next door. 'I was going to show you how to make these flowers.'

Eileen put an arm round her shoulder, feeling humbly guilty and said to their old friend, quietly, 'Don't go Ethel. We have to make our own fun. We seldom have anything to laugh at. But it was not at you. It was with you.'

Ethel sat down again. 'The dried egg is for you, I put one of the packets on the sideboard. That's why I made him the socks, you see.'

Jim Blake had given the girls a chicken for Christmas dinner. His Mum sent a plum pudding which contained one or two clean silver three-penny pieces inside. It was fun seeing who had one in her slice of Christmas pudding.

Jim did not join them, as he said he couldn't leave his mother and her sister Nell, who always spent Christmas with the Blake's.

The two girls asked Ethel and George to come round and join them, so they shared their roast chicken. During the evening they played cards, dominoes, and George went next door and got his dartboard, so they ended their very happy evening playing darts.

George was like a brother to them. Well, they had gone to school together, and had grown up mates. He did have a soft spot for Ann and through their teens they had gone dancing at the Chapel Street Hall together on a Saturday night. George went out a lot with a girl from Sholing, whom he had met at the dance one night, so they drifted apart. The romance, however, did not last and he went back to calling in for Ann to go to the cinema with him. Ann was shy and their friendship had been a slow-go one ever since.

The dance hall had been bombed, also two of the picture houses. However, most of the young girls had joined the Armed Forces, and the boys had been called up for Service at eighteen. The ones that were left had to go out of town for evening entertainment and had to walk miles, as the buses or trams did not run after ten o'clock at night.

On New Year's Eve, the two girls went to Beech Cottage for tea. Jim took them in his local farmer's small van. Mrs Blake made them so welcome, and took to Ann who did feel a bit awkward, knowing that her sister would have preferred to be on her own with Jim. But Eileen did not feel happy about leaving her behind, not on the last day of the year.

As they rode out of town they could see the fire still burning in the docks. The big sheds that all the butter was stored in had burned for three days already. The melting fat running in streams could not be put out. The fire was like an enormous melted candle. The enemy bombers had picked a sensitive target, like they did at the sugar factory. Nearly impossible to put out. The intense heat too was dreadful for the firemen. The Southampton firemen were so brave.

Martha Blake was well-liked and had many friends. She and Jim's father had a smallholding for many years. They also ran the tiny Post Office when Jim was a small child, from Beech Cottage. But just before the nineteen thirties Joe had died, leaving her a widow and too many strings. She retired and after selling a few animals had given her time to bring up her little son, Jimmy.

She was pleased to meet Ann for the first time and stared at her for quite a few seconds, then, releasing Ann's hand at last, she just said, 'Incredible!' Eileen saw the look on Mrs Blake's face and filled in the blank moment with a smile and said to the older woman. 'Yes! We are alike. You see we're identical twins.'

'Oh my goodness!' Mrs Blake looked first at Ann then at her son. 'You are doubly lovely. Now please make yourself at home, girls. Come and sit by the fire.'

It became a lovely day. Somehow Ann did not feel so much the odd one out. Jim had found a soft cushion for her neck and he had pulled her chair out for her when they sat at the table with the snow-white cloth on for tea.

Ann asked her if the gorgeous lace edging on the cloth was her handwork. 'Did you do this?'

'Yes,' she said. 'I learned lace-making as a child. It is a nice hobby. I'll show you how to make it one day. That is if you'd like to learn?'

Ann in her flush of eagerness was just about to answer, 'Oh, yes!' but in that second she had caught a glimpse of her sister Eileen's face. It was like the park notice, 'Keep Off the Grass', so she simply said, 'I couldn't, not now. You see my hands are now tough. Gardener's hands.' Nervously she slid them under her. It was the moment to change the subject, as Mrs Blake went on to ask the girls about their jobs. She saw Eileen's face too. 'I know that you're a nurse, Eileen. Yes! Healing hands. You have lovely, soft hands, you know and Ann,' she looked at her again, 'where do you garden, dear?'

Ann told her, and it felt nice to just tell someone about her new job. Her enthusiasm gave her face a glow.

'You're working for young Dobbs in Wick Lane. He has six greenhouses. You know his flowers are cut, packed and sent up to London on the eight o'clock train. No tomatoes yet. It is too early for them,' Mrs Blake continued. 'The nurseries are only ten minutes' walk from here; I shall see more of you.'

Ann sat quietly as she did not want to look at her sister or Jim. She suddenly felt as if the sun had gone from the sky. It had been silly to think that she could be only ten minutes away from Jim's mother when she finished work. No! She must not intrude on Eileen's world. A sudden stab of feeling made her realise, it was not her sister's world, but Jim's that she would intrude into.

Ann drew back a little and let the conversation dwell on her sister and Jim. She had difficulty in stemming the flow of self pity creeping through her thoughts. She was hungry for love. The thought of someone taking her hand, or putting a strong arm around her, gave her a warm feeling.

Mrs Blake looked across the table at her. 'You're quiet, Ann.' She smiled as she said it. 'Would you like another cup of tea?'

Ann looked up and their eyes met for a brief moment. 'No, thank you. I've had enough. It was a lovely tea. You're very kind to invite me.'

'I would! Like another cup of tea, please.' Eileen's voice was as soft as silk. Jim placed an arm around her shoulder. 'Right my love, I'll make a fresh pot,' he said, getting up.

'Thank you, son.' Mrs Blake's face was inscrutable as she put a shovel of coal on the fading fire. 'Do you know, Ann, there are stars in the night sky and a moon. At last, a moon. It's a clear night. Hope the air raids don't start.'

'The war time black-out makes it so dark,' Ann remarked. 'The moon will help us see our way home. Do you know it's difficult for my sister, she is often out late. She does night shift at the hospital. The Germans bombed the hospital, you know.'

Mrs Blake stopped what she was doing and looked at Ann. 'Your sister works hard, she is a brave girl. You both have to go out in the dark mornings to work. Oh, and don't worry about getting home tonight. Jim has the loan of Bill Webb's van. He brought you and will take you back in it. He's a nice man. Jim does a few little odd jobs for him on his time off.' She leaned across and whispered in Ann's ear. 'I don't think he'll get time now, do you?' She gave a little laugh, as if it was a secret between them.

Eileen and Jim cleared the table and while they were out in the kitchen, Mrs Blake came across and sat by the fire with Ann.

'While they're washing up the cups and plates we'll warm ourselves by the fire and chat,' she said. 'It's been so quiet lately. Do you think we shall get some more air raids?' she asked Ann. 'It makes you uneasy. You find yourself waiting and listening for the sound of aircraft. I know we don't get the bombs,' she went on, 'but we hear them. It's only a few miles away, Southampton.' She leaned closer to Ann. 'You know you can come here if we do. I can make room. Don't forget there's refuge here.'

'Thank you for your kind thought,' replied Ann softly. 'But we have to manage. You can't run away. We know what it's like. It's no stranger.'

'Another thing,' said Mrs Blake, 'I'm so sorry about your mother, and your granny. Have you any other family?'

Ann shook her head. She found it difficult to talk about it. It was too soon.

'Call me Ma,' said Mrs Blake, getting away from sad moments. 'My name is Martha actually, and I think Ma would be nicer than keep calling me Mrs B. I can't ask you girls to call me Mum, not yet, if ever. You cannot replace a Mum.'

'What's this about Mum?' Eileen came in from the kitchen followed by Jim.

'Just a suggestion that you girls call me Ma. It is a little bit formal calling me Mrs Blake. My Christian name is Martha.'

Eileen didn't reply for a minute but looked at Ann then the mask of indifference slipped and with a soft smile she said, 'I shall call you Martha, I think it is such a lovely name.'

'Yes. That's fine. Now I must go to the larder and get you girls the pie I made for you. Be nice for tomorrow,' she said.

Ann looked up at the old railway clock on the wall. It was ten o'clock and time they went home. Jim looked at her, and nodded approval. He went to get their coats.

The journey back to Southampton was enchanting. The moon shone on the Forest, through the leafless trees and the evergreen patches of bare grass while the gorse seemed to have become a hiding place for wildlife. Rabbits sat in the road then the next minute they were gone. In spite of bombs and a troubled world, life went on.

The moment they drove through the town the scenery underwent an eerie change: Ghost-like shells of empty burnt-out buildings formed rows of desolation, like a theatre play with the spotlight from the moon on the actors.

A few people were still out in the town but the silence was suddenly broken by the noises coming from one of the very few pubs left in the city. A small crowd of people were thronging around the door with their beer glasses, mugs or jam jars in their hands. The cause of the excitement was no doubt because the drayman had been with the beer. It was a well-known fact that people followed the horses and wagon all around the roads until he stopped, then they knew the focal point of delivery. The beer was here! News travelled fast, but only one pub at a time would be lucky; the others would be next if they were on the delivery list. Glasses of course were in short supply. It was not only the windows of the pub that were shattered by the bombs: If you were not the object of a direct hit during an air raid, then the blast of your neighbour's bomb could end your supply of glasses or mugs. One such pub had a notice up on their boarded windows saying, 'Beer here today. Bring your own glass.'

Jim saw the girls home to the door, but would not go in. He made his way quickly back to the Forest with the big yellow moon all the way. He was stopped once by a Home Guard but they knew each other, so he continued on, listening now to the noise in the sky. Planes droned overhead all night until the early hours of the morning but they did not drop a single bomb. They went on to a further target, many miles away; there was nothing left worth bombing in Southampton as the factories had moved out to the outskirts of the city.

Jim tapped his mother's bedroom door when he got in. He was late. It took him time to get the borrowed van back to Bill. He knew his mum would worry. As it was, she was not asleep, but listening to the drone of engines as the planes went over. She was frightened for the girls. She loved them both. Both so alike, yet both so different.

It was a crisp, cold morning with the moon still reluctant to go. Jim was up early and rode his bicycle to work. Although it was not yet daylight he enjoyed the ride through the edge of the Forest, which he knew like the back of his hand. He had a quick word with the station master when he got there. There were a few people about so he did not refer to the meeting at the Civic Centre but he did notice that he still had the little pin brooch with R.W. on. Jim had remembered to put his on, not with any enthusiasm but with the sudden thought of it being for his country. It was a means of communicating and sharing his knowledge with the secret army.

Jim did not know that contact would be so soon: He got into Waterloo on time after a few changes and had no difficulty in spotting the people who had boarded the train at Southampton West. What he did notice were the extra men at the ticket barriers. They were checking Identity Cards and rail passes so no-one could rush. It was orderly. There was one man as usual; the second one was standing to attention by his side, and not in rail uniform. Probably police, plain clothes detective, thought Jim. No-one seemed concerned. He heard one remark 'Blooming war'. There were soldiers everywhere and other members of the Forces.

Jim waited on the footplate. His mate remarked on his lack of hurry for his flask of tea.

'God! You still short of sugar in your 'ouse?' he said, as he watched Jim suddenly hurrying to the tea buffet.

The usual little blonde girl knew what he needed. She took the flask from him and put some sugar in it. He had a small rock cake as well which lived up to its name. She laughed at him and said, 'Well you must be bloomin' hungry.'

If she had only known! Jim had spotted a woman who had stared hard at him a few minutes' ago. She had followed him to the tea buffet. He walked back towards the train with his flask and cake. The crowd had thinned out and he could feel someone walking behind him. She spoke, so he had to turn round. Their eyes met again as she asked, 'Can you help me? I seem to be on the wrong platform, but I don't know which number I need.'

'Depends which line. Where do you want to go?' he asked, politely. He stared into a lovely pair of brown eyes, fringed by long black lashes. She smiled and he now noticed how nice looking she was. She was tall and slender. People began milling around them, walking towards the station waiting room.

Her face leaned towards him and she whispered, 'Raise your arm, point to the right and say in a clear voice my directions quickly.'

Jim for the first time in his life was both puzzled and annoyed. He did what she asked and she kept up the strange conversation between her teeth.

'I saw your pin R.W. I'm also a Rail Worker or Rail Watch. We're looking for a German. He has a small boy of eight years old with him. The boy is a fake grandson. He is not so much a grandfather as he looks. He's about thirty six, wearing a long tweed overcoat and a trilby hat. If he boards your train, which he will, tell the station master at Southampton at once.'

Jim continued to give her directions, pointing to the other lines and in a flash she picked up her small black bag and suitcase and hurried away.

'Thank you so much for your help,' she shouted.

He went to his engine where Bob was putting coal in the furnace.

'You got caught, mate!' he said with a wry grin. 'I always say I don't know if they ask me.'

'Well, that's all right for you,' Jim replied, 'but the poor woman was lost. She asked a porter and he told her wrong.'

'Did you get your sugar?' asked Bob.

Jim muttered that he had but was looking along the platform. It was then that he spotted the man and boy about to board his train. They were four carriages from the engine. He moved back beside Bob and took out his flask and enjoyed his tea.

'You ain't got much time,' Bob grinned. 'Can I have your cake?'

'Yes! And shut up, will you? We got three minutes.' Waterloo was the biggest station in the south east and as such, was a great piece of engineering, with so many lines and junctions. The most interesting part about it was the station itself: The wrought iron gates were a work of art, and the barriers. Jim had always loved it.

As soon as they reached Southampton Jim made contact with the station master. The man and boy left in a taxi. The station master took the taxi number.

Jim left it there. He did not have time to tell him that his contact has been a woman. He was quite sure she was genuine. He told the detectives that. The only thing that irritated him was that he kept thinking about her, especially those lovely brown eyes.

'Damn the woman!' he muttered under his breath.

After weeks of trying they never discovered the whereabouts of the man and boy. The taxi driver was never seen again. He was a single man, living in a single rented room, dirty, with no personal possessions and not missed. The taxi firm had never employed him, and denied knowing him. It was a strange event, melting into the background of wartime.

Jim had forgotten all about the man and boy until a few weeks later. Even then the sudden jolt of memory did not stir his enthusiasm. He certainly did not connect it with the five men who got off his train at Waterloo, one day. It was the station master who told him over a pint in the pub called the Wheatsheaf Tavern that evening.

A trifle more keen of eye than Jim, he said that they were two of the fishermen who were pulled out from the sea weeks ago, he was sure. They had bought tickets for London and had gone on Jim's line. It had been quite legal, as they had their Identity Cards, train passes, and papers from a fishing company employing three men. He remembered them but wondered where the third man was.

Jim asked him if they had the same identification this time from London. He saw them board the train, but thought they were businessmen, or Forces on leave. They had plain clothes and each had a fawn colour raincoat. They had remained on their own, each one in a separate carriage. Jim had thought there was nothing unusual in that, in fact, they all had grey or white hair now, so he did not recognise them. But the station master had been at the barrier and had seen those features up close. The grey hair was false, he insisted. Jim drew the conversation to an end and picking up his bike, he made his way home.

Eileen and his mother were in the kitchen chatting when he got in. A kiss on the cheek for Mum and then Eileen was in his arms. He was pleased by her visit to his mother and he told her so.

They sat together at the table and Martha came in with a big pot of rabbit stew. The smell was delicious and they enjoyed the meal in a kind of companionable silence. Every now and then Jim would touch Eileen's hand and smile across the table at his mother at the same time. His happiness was brimming over. Soon afterwards Eileen prepared to leave for home. It was time. This time she had her own lift back, as her sister Ann had worked overtime as planned, and the nursery's van of Mr Dobbs took the girls back together. Ann had asked Joe, the driver to call at Beech Cottage so that she could see Ma for a few seconds and pick Eileen up at the same time.

It was a lovely end to a day, a war time day too but they were not to know that it would be the last happy gathering for a while to come.

They were also quite unaware of the changes about to disrupt their lives and leave them in a fog of fear and despair.

Chapter 8

It was a cold night, but the sky was full of stars. With no moon and no street lights because of the blackout, it was dark. There seemed to be a hush over the town, an eerie silence. No-one walked the streets and Southampton lay like an empty shell. Only the old Bargate stood firm, ageless. The people were afraid and the fear was heightened by the rumours gathered from an underground movement. Air raids were about to start again, fiercer, heavier bombs, they had said. Families got ready to use the damp cold air raid shelters again and then as night wore on, they crept out and went back to their beds.

Eileen and Ann were tired after a long working day so they had agreed to sleep in the house. Ann peered through the crack in the curtains, looking from her bedroom window.

'It's a sort of ghostly silence,' she said to her sister who came in to say goodnight. It was ten o'clock, not too late.

'Yes!' said Eileen a little sharply. 'If they think we're waiting in fear, then they don't know British people. I don't think they'll bomb again. After all, there isn't much left of importance to the enemy.'

Ann gave a sigh of relief, as if any statement from Eileen would be right. She knew. 'That's what I think. Did you know,' she continued to chatter as she slipped into her bed, 'they've moved the factory further up country in to small sections? Even the Spitfires are now being built in parts, in garages, smaller buildings.'

'Well, I am going back to bed. Goodnight Sis,' said Eileen, more kindly this time, amused at her sister's chatter.

Ann lay quietly waiting for sleep to take over. It took an awfully long time. The last time she looked, the bedside clock showed the time was 11 o'clock.

Eileen too lay awake for hours. She had been the one to make preparations for a flying visit to the Anderson Shelter. Shoes, warm coats for her and Ann and a flask of hot tea. But sleep took over, and in the silence of that night the two girls let their dreams fill their tortured minds and let the angry world outside remain a stranger.

Perhaps it was just as well that the twins were totally unaware of what was about to happen that night. As the town of Southampton slept, history was being made. The very thing that everyone feared was about to happen. There were of course night patrols on the dark, empty streets, police, Home Guard, air-raid wardens and the Observer Corps but even they were unaware of the impending danger. It was quiet, except for an occasional voice calling out to a mate.

'Quiet tonight, Bill.'

'Yeah. They ain't comin' tonight. They be gone to Hitler's funeral I guess.'

'Now now, wishful thinking Joe.' The laughter died away with his footsteps.

Eileen was the first one up. It was six o'clock and she was on early call at the hospital at six thirty. It was a good shift as she would finish at twelve thirty, with time at home. She was lighting the fire when Ann came in the kitchen in her dressing gown. The days were still cold and her first shock had been to find that the coal bunker was empty. The only coal was in the small bucket. Her heart had sunk but she still put a match to the paper and sticks and decided that a small fire was a must!

Anne's face was white and she spoke in a shaky voice. 'They're here!'

'Who?' Eileen looked at her sister's face. 'Who? For goodness sake, just go and get dressed.'

Ann's voice had a slight squeak. She moved closer to her sister and gripped her arm. 'The Germans! I saw them.'

'You what?'

'I saw them, lots of them. Some in the headlights of a car or a lorry. Others creeping about on the dark side of the road. Come to the front of the house and see out of the front windows. See for yourself. Come on!'

Still reluctant to believe her sister, Eileen followed. 'It's too quiet, Ann. German boots and coarse voices would make a noise.'

They pulled aside the curtains in the best room and looked out on to the road. It was only five past six and still dark outside. What they saw made their hearts beat fast with fear. The road was like a theatre with puppets on a string, as so many shadowy figures kept bobbing up and down by the fronts of the houses. Here and there a beam of light would light up the men's steel helmets. There were at least thirty or forty soldiers in control of the area. It was like a nightmare, because with it all, there had been no sound. The stillness was so intense as to be unnatural.

The twins came together, arms around each other. In a whisper that held terror, Ann said. 'Do you think they'll come in the houses? Shall we let them?'

Eileen's voice was quite calm. 'Yes! I dare say. But stop and think. We let them in. You understand. No locking doors. It's bloody cold without a door. They would only break it down to come inside. So what is the point? Ann! Bear this in mind and keep it inside of you. They're not invited – and won't be allowed to stay here for long. Come on back to the kitchen, it's so cold in this room.'

'I don't want any breakfast.'

'Well, you're having some, whether you like it or not.' Eileen made two bowls of porridge and with eyes that glared at Ann, she sat down and dared her to leave it.

They got ready for work in a dream, as if it were just another normal day. They would go to work as usual.

A tap at the back door left them speechless. Both girls stood transfixed. With shaky fingers Eileen unbolted the back door. Mrs Sharpe took one step inside and broke down in tears. They could do nothing with her for a few minutes. When she could find her voice, she related to the girls all what happened in the last few minutes.

She had been out in her coal shed with a torch, trying to find enough coal to light a fire. A German had seen her because of the beam of light from her torch. She had turned round and found him standing in there.

'He didn't hurt me,' she said. 'In fact, he was kind and carried the coal scuttle into the kitchen. But he told me not to go out. He said they wanted the road clear. It was a curfew until we were told different.'

'What about going to work?' asked Ann in amazement.

'I asked him that, because George is still in bed. They don't go into work until seven thirty,' she said between tears. 'He said, "You all stay in your houses for one day. No work."'

'Oh!' said Ann. 'Well! That's it.'

Mrs Sharpe got up from her chair to go. As she was going she suddenly said 'He had a gun in the holster on his belt.'

Eileen got prepared to go to the hospital as soon as it was daylight. She talked it over with Ann and decided that the Germans would give her permission, on the grounds that at sometime one of their own soldiers may get sick or shot. Like us they all needed the hospital, nurses and doctors. It was wishful thinking. She could imagine Dr Shaw and Dr Preston putting a needle in them.

At eight o'clock she put her thick coat on top of her nurse's uniform, picked up her bag and went out the front door. There were soldiers at every corner and she felt sick with fear. The first one shouted at her, pointing his rifle, 'You were told to stay in your house.' His hostility showed in his whole body. His face lined with anger, he stopped her dead in her tracks.

Eileen turned to go back, all her courage gone with the wind. She had failed to do the things she set out to do.

'Halt!' His loud harsh voice pierced the silence. 'You will go when I say so on my orders. Not before!'

He kept her standing still for several minutes, in the cold. It was a light frost, but enough to glisten white on the garden gates. If it had not been for another German soldier coming to see what was happening, Eileen felt sure that she would have been made to stand there for ever.

She looked at him. He was of a higher rank and when he spoke it eased her fear. His voice was soft and his English was perfect.

'Where are you going?' he asked. 'You did know you are not allowed on the roads until the curfew is off.'

'No! I didn't know.' She gave him a smile of innocence. 'Actually,' she added, 'I am a nurse at the hospital. I should be at work.' As she spoke, she was unbuttoning her coat, to reveal her uniform.

'In that case I apologise. It is important work. If you will wait there I will get a car and take you. It is too dangerous to walk streets today. Tomorrow will be better.' He said something in German to a soldier then went swiftly up the road towards an army staff car. When he came back he made her sit in the front by the side of him.

'I am Heinrich Shultz,' he said quietly. 'You ask for me if you have any trouble. I do not want hatred or bad things to happen. I want people to understand that we will not harm anyone. If you do what we say, you will have food and freedom to go to and from your homes. We do not intend to keep you prisoners, only if you fight us.'

Eileen was stunned. Had he forgotten, they were uninvited and intruders, also it was war and they were our enemies.

He drew up to the front of the hospital. Another shock, he knew where it was. Eileen felt weak at the knees as she got out of the car.

'You have not told me your name,' he asked.

'Nurse Smith,' she said coldly.

'Ah! Please give my high regards to Matron,' he said. 'And Nurse Smith, I shall pick you up and take you home at three o'clock your time.'

The next minute he was gone, leaving Eileen wondering if it was all a dream.

When she entered the hospital everything seemed the same as usual. The doctors were there, also Matron, but Eileen was the only nurse in the whole building. They all met in Matron's office to discuss the work schedule, and the shocking situation. Each one of them vowed to continue nursing the sick and the dying.

As they made their way to Matron's office, Doctor Shaw gently took Eileen's hand and whispered, 'Are you all right?'

She squeezed his long, soft fingers, then the moment was gone, Matron was already in the chair.

'How did they get here? It was all so ghastly quiet.' said Doctor Shaw.

Doctor Preston had a faint smile across his lined face. A brisk interruption from Matron as she remarked sourly, 'I fail to see anything amusing in that question, Doctor.'

'Sorry Matron, but we were all fooled into waiting for an air raid, while all the time they were creeping up the Solent in a neutral ship, with a cargo of food on board, only the 'food' was German soldiers crammed in to the hold like sardines in a tin.'

How on earth do you know all this?' asked Matron. Doctor Preston looked a little smug as he related his story involving his neighbour who was in the police force and had been on dock duty.

'Why wasn't he captured?' asked Eileen.

'Because he was late on duty and managed to get away before the fun really started.'

'And you expect us to believe that?' said Matron. 'I can't see any point in this conversation,' she added with a grim look at the doctor. 'Now we have two wards here full of patients. The poor things have had no food, no bed strip, no wash and no dressings changed on their wounds. We must work all together the four of us. A third of the hospital is gone, only rubble left after the last raid. So we make the best of it.' Matron's face was flushed with anger. Everyone stared at her outburst.

'Yes! You lot,' she said. 'Come on, let's surprise the German army. Let's get on as if they are not there. Oh, and by the way, have any entered the building yet?'

'Yes,' said the doctor. 'An officer appeared in the entrance hall a while ago but I told him about the virus.'

'What virus?' said Matron, towering over him.

'You know,' he smiled, 'the killer one in Ward Nine. Well, he hurried out quicker than he came in. He cursed a few times in German. I know what he said. He was quite unaware that I understood the language.'

Eileen made her way to the Wards with a heavy heart. Some of the other nurses lived a bus-ride away and with no buses on the streets today, she was the only one of them to have arrived for work. She had no idea how they were going to manage with only one nurse, two doctors and the Matron. It was fortunate that both doctors had been on night duty and were already there and that Matron lived at the hospital, otherwise she would have been alone. They would have to pull together, thought Eileen in despair.

She worked on all through the day and was exhausted when she signed off duty. The thought of the walk home frightened her but as she walked down the steps at the front of the hospital a taxi pulled up beside her and the driver called out to her. 'Get in miss. I've got instructions to take you home. You are Nurse Smith?'

'Yes.' She almost fainted and closed her eyes for a moment as she got into the taxi. She was worried about Ann.

'Captain Heinrich Shultz sent me to collect you.' Eileen got in the cab and he said, 'You will have to tell me where you live, Miss.'

She felt a strange mixture of disappointment, anger and humiliation but inside deep guilt at even thinking about him and the ride back sitting close to him. He smelled of after-shave and expensive soap. His hands on the wheel had been tanned but soft, with finely cut and polished nails. He spoke such perfect English that you would not know he was German, except for his uniform.

'Is this the road, Miss?' The taxi driver broke up her chain of thoughts.

'Yes, it's number seven.'

'Not many houses left in this road,' he said as he opened the taxi door for her.

'No! Nor people. It took them as well. Sixteen,' she added and as she put the key in the door to number seven there were tears running down her cheeks.

Ann was in the kitchen and peeling a large potato. She rushed to her sister and hugged her. 'Dear Sis! I've been thinking about you all day.'

Eileen sank into the nearest chair. She was so tired that nothing touched her any more. 'We'll sit and talk after tea. What we got?'

'Mashed potato and I found a tin of corned beef.' Ann got the opener out of the kitchen drawer and got the tin of corned beef open, but in the process she cut her finger. She grabbed the tea cloth and set her mouth in a tight line, as she wrapped it round her hand. It bled quite a bit.

Eileen got up from her chair and looked at it. 'You silly bitch, what did you do that for? Don't you think I have seen enough blood for one day,' she shouted.

Tears and sobs mingled with 'Sorry!' blotted out the whimper from Ann. 'I didn't do it on purpose, Sis.'

There is only so much a person can take. The shock, pain, the world so upturned, even the home life. No coal, little food. The girls wept in each other's arms.

Ann spoke first. 'Come on let's finish having our cuppa tea, then we'll finish cooking the spuds.'

She went to the coal bucket and took out wood for the fire. 'I had to chop up those old chairs out in the shed for firewood. The coal was finished, only dust left.' She attempted a laugh. 'Mrs Sharpe said we could make briquettes with it! She said mix it with something.'

Eileen looked up at her sister. 'Glad we had those old chairs, anyway, I think there may be one or two more bits for the chopper before long, don't you?'

'Makes a good fire. Sooner have it than dirty coal.' Suddenly they were both laughing, the cut finger forgotten.

When they had eaten their meal Eileen told her sister of the day's work and lack of staff, and the patients.

'How did you get there?' asked Ann. 'I take it they didn't try to stop you.'

'Oh, no. I had a lift after I said I was a hospital nurse.'

'A lift in what?'

'A German soldier gave me a lift to work.'

'You didn't sit next to him?' said Ann in horror.

'Yes. He was polite and it was the only answer. Look, there was no one on the roads only Germans. I had to keep my temper and my mouth shut. I got there.'

'How did you get back?'

'Taxi,' said Eileen. 'The same German sent a taxi for me.' She suddenly laughed. 'Do you know what Doctor Preston told the German?'

'No!'

'Well, he said we had an infection, a killer, in Ward Nine. The German soldier went out quicker than he came in. They have left us alone all day.'

Ann looked at Eileen in amazement, before she so innocently asked, 'Do you really have this awful infection at the hospital?'

'Good grief, no! Of course not! No more than we have a Ward Number Nine, silly! But it kept them out. We don't want them inside of the hospital because it would frighten the patients. At the moment they don't know anything. You see, Ann, this is one occasion when a little knowledge might be a dangerous thing. Now tell me what you have been doing all day.'

'Wondering how Martha and Jim are, and if they are safe.'

Eileen felt guilty at not giving more thought to Jim. 'Will you try and get into work tomorrow, Ann?' she asked.

'Yes. If they stop me and send me back here, well that's it. Then again, the nurseries may no be allowed to pick us up if we do get as far as the Bargate. What a mess, Eileen. I'm glad Mum isn't here. It would have killed her anyway! I won't sleep tonight. Will you? With all those soldiers about everywhere. There was fighting in the road today. I looked out of the front window and down the road people were using knives and even garden forks. It was stupid as the soldiers had rifles. Let's take a hot water bottle and go to bed. The fire is going out and we mustn't waste that wood.'

'No, it won't last long,' answered Eileen.

'Let's put the lights off and go on up to bed then. Get the hot water bottles first. I hope Jim and Ma are safe.'

'Stop it,' said Eileen. 'I can't cope with the worry.'

It was not a quiet night. Ann could hear scuffles in the road. Shots were being fired and the dreaded sound of heavy gunfire rattled in the distance. She did not sleep. Eileen was in the back of the house and she did sleep. It was the sleep of exhaustion.

Chapter 9

Jim Blake woke early and cycled through the Forest to the station. It was still dark in the mornings, but the sky was clear and the stars shone. There was no moon and the only sound in the Forest was from the sudden movement of a fox, or a pony. He loved the journey to work at daybreak.

When he reached Southampton he had a shock to see people, shadowy figures in and out of doorways and his heart nearly stopped beating when he heard a sharp voice somewhere behind him, call out, 'Who goes there? Stop!'

He did just that. His body stood rigid. The face came nearer and he stared in the half-light at a soldier in a German helmet.

'Where are you going? Who are you?' the soldier asked.

'I'm a railway worker. A train driver,' he answered with a pang of fear in his stomach.

'Show me your card,' he demanded, shining a torch on Jim.

Jim reached in his pocket for his Identity Card, but a large, coarse hand reached his pocket first, taking out the contents. He then ran his fingers over the rest of the pockets.

'No gun. Good, you can go,' he said in perfect English. He handed Jim back his ID card. He kept the rest, a handkerchief, a pound note and a handful of small coins.

Bewildered and shaken, he entered the railway station and looked for the staff but found that the only people there were soldiers. Germans!

The truth of the situation quickly sank in. They were here and had come in large numbers, had no doubt taken over the port. Jim suddenly wished for daylight but it was still only six-thirty. There were soldiers everywhere; they had taken over the station and it was deadly quiet.

There should have been the Southampton to Weymouth train on the other line, getting fired up ready for the journey at seven forty five and his own to Waterloo on the up line. Several more times Jim was stopped and they refused to let him out of the station when he tried to leave. He felt trapped, and wanted to be allowed to go home. The appearance of Bob his stoker brought a smile to his face.

'Thank God you're here, Bob. I can't get any sense out of this lot. What the hell's going on? Can you tell me?'

It took his mate some time to reveal the picture of life in the town, and suburbs.

'Have you any news of the hospital? I want to find out if Eileen and her sister are all right.'

'Well, I think so,' said Bob. 'But they only had one nurse turn up for work at the hospital apart from two doctors. This nurse had a lift in one of the German cars, sitting up there beside an officer. She was booed, my mate told me. Some girls will run after any man. He was a good looking bloke. Well ... for a German.'

Eileen would have stayed at home, Jim thought. She would be safe with Ann and their nice neighbour. It made Jim all the more determined to go and see her.

When the station master arrived for work he looked anything but happy. In fact, for such an immaculate little man, he gave the impression of having just scrambled out of bed. He produced a huge bunch of keys and opened his office door.

Jim followed him inside. "Where did all these Jerries come from?'

The Station Master nodded at Jim. 'Sit down lad,' he said quietly. 'The rumour is, a ship came into the docks late last night to unload a cargo of food, flying the flag of a neutral country it was. But there was no cargo of food. Instead, it was full of bloody Germans, waiting silently below decks, ready to take the harbour and the town. Officers on deck and in the wheel-house carefully disguised, papers all in order, with Irish accents and beaming smiles. Surprise was their weapon. They say it's the prelude to the main invasion still to come, a spearhead force to capture the port for the rest of the waiting invasion force. I've had my orders from the Germans: All trains in and out are cancelled. Later, maybe tomorrow, they'll be running troop trains up to the front line, north of Southampton and south as far as Lymington.' He looked at Jim and there was anger in his tone when he said, 'The railway's now in German hands and so are we!'

As he spoke he could hear the thump of heavy boots outside the door. Jim had been sitting quietly listening to him, but now he got to his feet and pulled open the door.

'Stay where you are!' shouted the soldier outside.

'Look, man!' said Jim. 'I'm going home. No trains. No work. I'm not staying here. I'll come back tomorrow.' He pushed past the soldier and headed for the outside. Two more stopped him, and he said the same to them, showing his I.D. card and keeping walking, conscious that they all had rifles. He reached the turnstile and went through. Still a free man.

At least he thought he was, until a car pulled up beside him on the pavement and a German officer shouted, 'Stop! You! Get in the car.'

Jim was shaken but did as he was asked. They moved away from the railway station, but didn't go through the town centre. They headed for Ramsay Street, then into Glenmore Road.

'There you are, Mr Blake. I believe you have a young lady friend here,' the officer said, stopping the car at number seven. 'Remember, you work for us now on the railway. Do you understand?' He looked straight into Jim's eyes and seeing Jim hesitate, his tone changed. 'Yes! Mr Blake. I will see to it that your young lady Nurse Smith is safe and looked after. But if not ... This road is not popular ...'

He didn't finish the sentence, but Jim had already got the message.

'I understand what you mean,' said Jim, as he got out of the car.

Jim never knew if he had heard him or not, the roar of the engine as he drove off was loud and very final.

Ann answered his knock on the door. She could not believe her eyes! Her face lit up in surprise and sheer wonder. She flung herself at him, hugging him closely. 'Jim, you're all right, it's so good to see you,' she said feeling slightly embarrassed at her action. She led him into the warm kitchen.

'Where's Eileen?' he said anxiously, looking around the kitchen. 'She's all right?' he demanded, his attitude changing.

'Eileen's gone to work,' Ann said with a worried look. 'She's still at the hospital and won't be home until five. They're seriously short of staff, in fact, there was only her and two doctors and Matron all day yesterday.'

'Ah! So she was the one, the only nurse there,' he answered curtly.

'Is something wrong?' she asked. It was not like Jim to sound so hollow, or be so curt with her.

Jim took her hand in his. 'I'm so sorry, Ann, I've got a lot on my mind at the moment. It's life-changing, I only hope I can cope for her sake.'

As he turned to leave she gripped his arm. 'You will help us, Jim,' she cried, 'You won't leave us?'

'No, tell Eileen I'm still working on the railway. Maybe a different job that's all. Now I must go and see if my mother is all right. You know, Ann, I didn't know we had been invaded this morning when I left home. It's so quiet in the country we didn't hear them. I rode my bike in. I've left it at the station. I shall have to go back for it. I've also got to collect a travel pass from the Germans they said, so I can leave Southampton to go home.'

Long after he had left number seven he began to wonder if he should have told Ann the full story. There was a mystery surrounding that German officer. How did he know Nurse Smith, or her address, or his relationship with her?

'Your lady friend, Nurse Smith,' he had said, so smugly.

The journey back through the Forest was strange. He passed German patrols on the road and expected to be stopped at any moment. When he reached their cottage Jim's mother met him at the door, "Jim, it's the invasion! Are you all right? I've seen German soldiers in the village. What are we going to do?'

It took him some time to get her settled by the fire. He didn't keep anything from her and told her about the German officer. She listened carefully and agreed to keep it a secret, even from the girls. Martha realized that her son either worked with the enemy or got shot. But worse still was the underlying hint of blackmail. Jim had to drive the trains, or take the consequences. This German had him over a barrel. 'Poor lad, what a load of stress to carry on young shoulders,' she thought sadly.

'How are the girls, Jim?' his mother asked.

'I only saw Ann,' he said. 'Eileen was still at work.'

'Son, if Ann came here, she could get to work at the nurseries easier. What do you think?'

'No! Mother, she wouldn't leave her sister. There's a bond between them.'

'Well, Eileen could come here too.'

'It's not as simple as that, Mum.'

'Why?' she asked.

'Well, if they leave the house, the Germans would take it over. All empty buildings are now being claimed.'

'What a pity, I would love Ann to live here to keep me company when you're at work. I got a bit scared today here alone.'

'Look, Mum, don't be frightened. I met Peter Young, on the way here. He's a Home Guard. We talked and I asked him to keep a watch on our cottage, see you are safe when I am not here.'

'Thank you, dear.'

Jim put his coat back on again.

'Where are you going now?' His Mum grabbed his sleeve.

'I'm going to Wick Lane Nurseries to find out what's happening. Ann has not heard from them. She has to have transport to get to work. She's worried.'

'All right, Jim, don't be long then!'

Wick Lane was quiet. No sign of life. There was a strange emptiness about the place when Jim arrived. The nurseries gates were locked, but there was the small path around the side to reach the house. It was a large, brick house with tiled roof. The nursery owner had it built when he married. He had planned it around a family, four bedrooms and a nursery, five rooms down, counting his music room. Cliff Dobbs was a lover of Big Band music. His one great heartache was that they had no children. Years of waiting left him cold towards his lovely wife. That was the cause of rumours around the villages of his liking for women. He had been involved with his secretary for the last year.

Jim Blake rang the bell and waited. He began to wonder if the house was empty. In fact, he had turned to retrace his steps when Cliff opened the door.

'Hello Mr Dobbs,' said Jim.

'Ah! It's Jim Blake isn't it? Come on in!'

Jim followed him to a small sitting room at the back of the house. It was small but cosy with a wood burning fire. A small table in the window had a white cloth and a half-eaten meal on a plate.

'Sorry if I've interrupted your supper,' said Jim.

'It doesn't matter. Anyhow, it was cold. Nothing matters.' His voice was so quiet and loaded with despair. Jim was amazed at the change in him. He was so tempted to find out why. This was really the time for inner strength and courage. People were battling with their anger and hatred. To survive you had to grin and bear it for the time being anyway. Cliff had buckled. He looked beaten.

'Well, Cliff, I've come about one of your workers, Ann Smith. I know she'd only just started here to work in your nurseries but she can't get here without transport. Are you going to send the pick up van for her? Or is she sacked?'

'What is she to you?' asked Cliff.

Jim looked him straight in the face. There was a hint of defence in his answer. 'She happens to be my fiancé's sister. They lost their parents, so they're living together in their old house. Ann needs the work. The other sister's a nurse. We have to survive!'

Cliff pulled himself up in his chair. His face changed colour. The white face now flushed with anger.

'Yes! Of course you are right, Jim. The only snag is ... cash. They've taken over the Bank. Really, I don't know what is going to happen about the wage system, or our finances. However, I'll keep Ann on and pay her out of my own pocket. I've known your family for donkey's years, Jim.

I'll also keep Joe on for the tomatoes. I'll put Ann in charge of the flower bulbs.'

Cliff had lowered his voice to a whisper. Jim thought it strange. Then he heard footsteps from above. Of course, Cliff's wife was upstairs in the bedroom. Jim now lowered his tone as he said, 'I must go now. Shall I tell Ann?'

'Yes! Do. I'll write down the time and hours if you hang on a minute. Cliff scribbled some words on a piece of paper, folded it up small and handed it to Jim who was going to unfold it when Cliff shook his head and, grabbing the note from Jim's hand, stuffed it down inside the front of Jim's shirt. 'Read it when you get home,' he whispered.

It was then that Jim knew the house, so silent, was not empty. As he left, he had the feeling that he was being watched. His keen eyes, trained to watch the railway line ahead for danger, saw the bedroom curtains flicker slightly. Nothing more. But when he got out into Wick Lane there were two German soldiers who stopped and searched him. They went through his pockets, but found nothing, only his I.D. card and rail card.

Mrs Blake was cooking a meal for them both when Jim came back home. 'You were a long time,' she said.

'Yes! I know. But I had a chat with Cliff Dobbs, and he's keeping Ann on, as long as the Germans let him.'

'That's good, love'. She was smiling as she dished up their tea.

'A nice piece of home-cured bacon,' she said.

'Where on earth did you get that?' Jim asked.

'From Bill. He popped down to see me this morning. He brought me this bacon and a little bit of butter.'

'What did he want?'

'He wants you to put a bolt on his kitchen door. On the inside. He said two German soldiers walked straight in, and Mary didn't have time to hide the butter she had just made. Of course, she had to give them some.'

'Didn't make any difference, they would have forced her to,' said Jim bitterly.

'Well, well!' said his mother, as she brought in a pot of tea. 'What are you reading? Did we have some post?'

'No! It's only a letter from Eileen,' he said, pushing the slip of paper into his shirt pocket. But as soon as she left the room he threw it in the flames of the fire. He didn't need it any more. Already it was stamped on to his mind. The message from Cliff Dobbs had read, 'My house is full of German officers. They have taken over the whole house. This is their hide-away. Secret. Keep it that way, for my sake. My wife is gone. No one missed her. She went to Oxford a week ago to her mother. She has left me.'

'Women! His mother didn't miss a trick,' he thought.

'What did you burn it for?' she said, looking at the tiny slip of paper left struggling to disappear.

'Love letters are for my eyes only,' he laughed.

'Well, I kept all of mine,' she said, looking at him lovingly. But Jim had closed his eyes and rested his head back. He could take no more.

Checking to see that his wife had gone to bed already, Bill Webb walked off through the Forest to the bunker. Most of

111

the men from his unit of the Auxiliary would be there tonight. Their officer was expected to brief them on the plans for future action. Bill had heard that British troops were mobilising at last in the North of England and were on their way south to engage the Germans. If they could push them towards the south coast, then they would have a chance of defeating them. Hitler had been mistaken in his calculations: After Dunkirk, he had thought that the British Army was obliterated but he was wrong. Bill's head whirled with a million thoughts: If only they knew how many German paratroops had landed. Lack of information was frustrating! His unit had lost their radio link with Middle Wallop but had received firm information about fierce pockets of resistance fighting the Germans three miles north of Southampton in several places.

He stopped to get his bearings under a large spreading oak, knowing that he was near the hideout. It was a cold night but of course it was early February. The night sky had been clear when he left the cottage but now, in the thick of the Forest it would have been easy to get lost.

Treading carefully, he listened intently for intruders in this part of the Forest: He rarely saw anyone but he had to be careful. Feeling around the trunk of the oak he found the opening. Yes, this was it. The old Forest giant was hollow right through the centre. A major storm would one day bring it crashing down. Taking three paces away from the tree, he took a small torch out of his pocket then ran his fingers through the leaf litter until he found what he was searching for, the edge of a wooden board. He lifted the edge of it carefully and smiled to himself as he lowered himself down into the hole beneath. Not many people have a roof garden, he mused. He climbed on down a wooden ladder, closing the trapdoor over his head as he did so. 'All right lads. It's Bill,' he said.

Ray Wicks put down his sten gun, not looking very happy. 'Blimey Bill. We weren't sure who it was. You thumped about a bit up there!'

Bill looked around the underground room, seeing six of his unit already there and their officer, Captain Downer. He was informal and salutes were not necessary. The Captain was a farmer who owned quite a lot of land to the west of the Forest, a good boss to work for, a brilliant regular army man from the First War.

The bunker was roughly ten feet square with the ladder fixed to one wall to save space. At the other end, a short tunnel led to a toilet area–a bucket! The room was already warm from the heat of their bodies and the tin walls glistened with beads of moisture. The men were sitting on a long wooden plank seat and there was a damp earthy smell pervading the room in spite of the corrugated iron sheets which lined the walls, keeping the earth sides from collapsing inwards. Stacked against the side wall were boxes and boxes of the very latest plastic explosives, detonators and reels of cable, enough destructive power, some of the unit reckoned, to blow up all the houses in the village. Other boxes held a large supply of tinned food; bread would not keep down there but the unit had supplies for several days if they were forced to 'go to ground'. One of the men owned the off-licence in the village and had hidden some of his spirits in the bunker when the invasion had started. He kept his mates supplied with 'warmers' as he called it. Ray also had a small radio transmitter with which they kept in touch with their base and with other units.

Captain Downer cleared his throat. 'Well now chaps, as we're all here now, let's get started. Ray has already told me that the news through the radio suggests that jerry is still pinned down north of Winchester thanks to our boys in the Royal Navy keeping them from crossing the Channel and landing heavy armour in Southampton docks. If the regular army can just keep up the pressure until proper reinforcements get down from up north, there's a good chance that he can be finally pushed back to the coast and beaten. In the meantime, the Eastleigh unit has been causing hell at the airfield, getting in under cover of night and blowing up their planes. The Ringwood lads have been doing the same at Stoney Cross and Ibsley airfields. They've been putting up a damned good show.

That leaves us doing our hit and run sorties on German patrols entering the Forest and our big chance to really hit back at jerry, we're going for the railway. I've given Ray the plan, drawn on rice paper, of course, with instructions that he's to eat it if he should get caught or be in trouble. Now this is what we're going to do ...'

The night wore on, the air in the underground bunker getting increasingly thicker, in spite of the fresh air filtering down from the air vent going up through the soil and coming out in the centre of the hollow tree. Bill heard a fox call out in the silent forest up above. Soon it would be dawn and the dead leaves would rustle with the movement of the forest animals. He had come to terms with the fact that any day could be his last, that the Germans would be ruthless with the members of the Auxiliary Units if they were ever caught. The men of the units were all of different ages and backgrounds; most were farmers, or farm workers and gamekeepers, men from reserved occupations who had not been called up and they all had two things in common, an intimate knowledge of the local area, particularly the New Forest and a willingness to die for their country if they had to.

Chapter 10

Jim slept heavily in the armchair. The fire had burnt low and Martha put a guard round what was left. She looked at her son and decided not to disturb him as, slowly, she had made her way up the stairs to her bed.

It was well past midnight when Jim woke up. A gentle tap on the kitchen window made him sit up. Drawing the curtain a tiny crease he could see a figure outside. The moon gave a soft light on him and he recognised his old mate and neighbour, Ray Wicks. Trying to be as quiet as possible, he slid the bolt on the back door and let him inside.

Ray looked flushed and agitated as he took the offered seat, drawing his breath before he spoke.

'What's up, mate?' said Jim softly.

'I had to see you!' whispered Ray. 'I just found out that you're going to be in terrible danger on the railway in the next few days. Our chaps are going to put explosives on the line. They're in action now Jim. You're not safe working on the railway. You'll have to work it that you're ill or something and can't go to work. Collapse. Make it look real.'

'Ray, I can't do that! They wouldn't buy it!'

'Could you jump off the footplate, after slowing down?'

'It's not a bloody bus! And I'd have to know where they put the explosives. No, it's impossible! I'll go for the sudden illness idea. But I'll have to think about it Ray. Have you forgotten my fireman? He'll have to go because I can't tell him anything.'

'No Jim. My God, you have my life in your hands and the rest of our unit, as well as your own. You know the drill. My mother would have a fit if she knew what I had joined! All those months when she thought I was out on patrol with the Home Guard and the nights we spent digging our hide-out in the woods. Jim, I have to go.'

'He said the girls would be safe. If not . . . It's blackmail to be sure but I have to go along with what he wants.'

Ray leaned forward and with eyes glaring angrily at Jim, he said, 'Who is this "he"?'

'He's an Officer! Heinrich Shultz. I should think he's in charge of Southampton and surrounding areas. The men all stand to attention when he's around.'

'Well! How come you got involved with him?' Ray said, his face grim. 'This old pal a collaborator?' His irritation grew by the minute. Jim put out his hand and grabbed Ray's.

'Please listen, hear my side of the situation, and don't spoil years of friendship for this. Hear me out.' Slowly with his voice still low, Jim told him the whole story. He even told Ray about the pin badge with R.W. on it. He told him how his plucky girlfriend Eileen Smith had gone to work just the same at the hospital, how she had walked up the empty road defying the Germans, then had a lift to work in the Officer's staff car.

'Yes!' said Ray,' now she's known as a collaborator.'

'Yeah! But she risked her good name to nurse those sick people in the hospital,' Jim replied sharply. 'By the way,' he went on, 'She's got a twin sister, Ann, who's working now for

Cliff Dobbs round at the nursery. She's going to keep Mum company three days a week. I worry about her alone in the cottage with me at work. She's an old lady.'

'You are still going into the station then,' muttered Ray.

'Yes. I'm going, even if my life's in danger. I made a promise to the Special Branch of the police. I have certain contacts to make for our sakes. The Germans think they have got us all licking their boots. But give us time and we shall get rid of them.'

'God! That was some speech,' said Ray, holding out his hand and giving Jim a beaming smile. 'Cheers.'

The two men shook hands in friendship and in silence. All that had been said this night would never leave the room.

A slight sound, no more than a swish of clothing made them both look round. In the doorway in her dressing gown, stood Jim's mother.

'Do you lads know it's three o'clock in the morning?'

Jim got to his feet. 'Yes, Mum, it's all right, we're only having a good old chat. Now you go back to bed and I'll see Ray out and lock up.'

'All right, son, but mind you bolt the door and turn the lamp out. Burning a lot of paraffin,' she muttered but it fell on deaf ears.

If only Jim had nothing worse to worry about than the price of oil for the lamps he would be a happy man, thought Ray Wicks as he walked home.

It took courage, patience, and a certain amount of fighting spirit to continue to run the small hospital. Matron had all these qualities but all the same, life was difficult. There were times when fear and anger rose to the surface, and she took vent on the nurses. A few had returned to work, but always in fear of being thought of as collaborators. Drug supplies had ceased, also the dressings, bandages, needles and syringes. The staff had resulted in washing the bandages that were not too caked in blood, and locking away the few bottles of clean fluids and disinfectant.

Doctor Preston caught a German stealing from the hospital drugs cupboard. Much to the amazement of his nurses he floored the German with one blow from behind. Matron screamed abuse and warned Doctor Preston of a possible retribution from the Germans

'We shall all be shot when they come looking for him, and they will, believe me!' she shouted. The soldier, still out for a count, was more dangerous to them than an active one. The Doctor dragged him out of the A&E room to the small side ward where they dropped him on to a bed. As fast as he could, the Doctor ran back for a syringe then he filled it and quickly stuck it into the soldier's arm, before he had time to recover. The drug he used would calm him. He then quickly undressed the German and got him between the sheets. One of the nurses put the necessary objects on his bedside table, while Doctor Preston made up a temperature chart at the foot of the bed. He added a few notes on his condition, and wrote 'Possible concussion. X-ray needed for head.'

It was far too serious to indulge in laughter, but Matron vowed she had never in her whole life seen such a pantomime. 'It's outrageous!' she muttered between clenched teeth. Doctor Preston put his finger to his lips.

He could see his patient was coming round. Blue eyes stared up at him and the nurse, a stare that was cold and calculating. The doctor went up to the side of the bed. Beneath his smile lay the certainty that this young soldier would be giving them no trouble. He probably would not remember.

'You won't remember anything,' he said quickly, knowing the soldier would have a job to understand.

Bending over him, he took his pulse, felt the glands in his neck, and nodded his head. 'You are a lot better,' he said, with a smile. He felt pleased with himself, and could not think of anything else to do that would convince this German. He called the nurse across to the bed and resuming his role of actor, said, 'Will you check his pulse every half hour. Bring him a bowl of soup and a piece of bread at one o'clock. Nurse Smith will be on duty soon, she will take over. By the way, Nurse, if anyone comes looking for him, tell them you found him passed out on the floor. Doctor thinks he may have suffered a fit. Come and get me at once. I will explain,' he said.

Once Doctor Preston had left, the nurse rebelled, storming into the big ward to declare her loyalty to her country. She was not going to nurse a German, an invader at that. She stamped her size four shoes on the wooden floor. Her face was flushed and angry. Matron, doing her usual rounds, heard what was going on. With a sudden swipe of her hand, she got hold of the nurse by her sleeve and marched her back to her office. There was a strange look on

Matron's face. What was said in that office that day, no one knew, or would ever know.

Back on the ward nurse Rose Trim, was at her best. She performed her sacred role of nursing at its best. She even nursed the German, taking him a cup of coffee and a bowl of soup at midday. When, at two o'clock, an officer of the German Army walked into the hospital, accompanied by two of his men, she went to fetch Doctor Preston as requested. She was scared.

The young soldier, sitting up in bed was quite obviously enjoying the fuss made of him. He kept thanking the nurse and the doctor, all in broken English, with a few phrases of German thrown in.

Doctor Preston could speak a little German so he approached the visitors with ease. Holding out his hand, he shook the hand of the German officer. There seemed to be a cauldron of fire inside of him as he took the hand of his enemy with a pleasant smile. The officer clicked his heels as he said, 'Heinrich Schultz. You have one of my men here, I am told. He was reported missing.'

'Doctor Preston, Sir.' As he spoke the nurse came up with the patient's chart and medical notes, written in German by the doctor. She handed them to Doctor Preston, then took the empty soup bowl and cup, and left them. Doctor Preston knew that the officer would ask to see the medical report so he handed it to him, pointing to the bed.

'Yes! One of your men is sick. This report explains it. It is in your language.'

'Oh! You need not have bothered, Doctor, I speak and work in your English language,' Heinrich said proudly.

Doctor Preston just nodded, and then said, 'Your man here does not! He was very confused at first, when he regained consciousness. I did this to reassure him that we are not harsh people. We save lives here, not take them.

'What exactly happened?' Heinrich asked.

Doctor Preston explained in medical terms, how a nurse saw him coming into the hospital and he suddenly went stiff, and fell backwards in a faint. 'She called me and I got him to bed. I did wonder if he was a diabetic, but I took a test and his sugar level was fine. Does he suffer with fits?'

Heinrich looked puzzled but refused to appear ignorant, so shook his head and said, 'No! My men are fit, more fit than your soldiers.'

'Right, well he can leave now. He seems to have recovered. He may find his head a bit sore, as of course he fell on his back on to the stone tiles at the entrance.'

'Well, thank you, Doctor, you have been most kind,' Heinrich said, holding out his hand. He nodded his head at the man in the bed, telling him to get dressed at once.

As soon as he was ready, the three Germans walked out of the hospital, but before they reached the entrance doors, Heinrich stopped and turned to Doctor Preston who was escorting them out of the reception area.

'Ah! Doctor. I ask you!' Heinrich's cold expression stirred the tiniest spark of fear in Preston's stomach. But he returned the look with a confident half-smile. 'What did the soldier come into the hospital for?' It was a deliberate turning of a situation, and the doctor knew he had to pull this one off with a little deep thinking.

'You must ask him,' Doctor Preston replied, casually. 'You know that some of your men have been admitted as patients, bleeding from knife wounds and shots. I took it that he may have been visiting a comrade. You must ask him.'

'I will, Doctor. I will. Thank you.' With a sudden click of his feet, the German officer and his men turned and left the building.

After they had gone, Doctor Preston looked for Matron. She was in a better mood and after laying down the law she praised him for handling the situation with such cool confidence. 'It could have turned nasty, especially when you floored him,' she said. 'Why on earth did you creep up on him and hit him on the back of the head? You were foolish, Doctor.'

'Well, matron, he was stealing our drugs. We are short of everything as it is. I just blew my top. Now I ask you, what alternative did I have? Tap him on the back and say, 'Caught you, you naughty boy.' He would have shot me first and then emptied the drug cupboard.'

Matron looked a trifle worried. 'Yes! In that case I must agree with you. But what if he talks?' she said anxiously.

'I don't think he's going to confess to that. That German officer was a strong character. He wouldn't steal. He would just take. There is a borderline of difference. I think he'll keep quiet, Matron. He didn't see the man who hit him. I made sure of that.'

Eileen had come on duty and she changed the sheets on the German's bed, unaware of the incident. Doctor Preston and Matron glanced at each other, but said nothing. He was a little troubled by Nurse Smith's growing friendship with Heinrich Shultz. He had noticed the staff car waiting outside to take her home as she came off duty. Doctor Preston did not miss much.

It was only eight o'clock when Eileen came off duty. Matron had promised her some short shifts as she was doing far too much. Her working hours had been way over the top. Two more nurses had come back to work now that the movement restrictions and the curfew had been lifted. People were free to return; however, trams, buses and vans had been taken off the road. Petrol was in short supply and was rationed. One taxi was allowed to run, but not out of town. Street fights had become fewer, as it all seemed pointless. If you fought your enemy – they shot you. It was as simple as that. Hundreds of propaganda leaflets had been posted on walls all over the town, warning people that they would not gain anything by fighting them. Food was on its way and would be distributed to all people who accepted their German friends. It was an evil time, setting people against each other. Family fist fights replaced the shooting.

Eileen left the hospital. Heinrich was not outside and it was dark, but the moon showed enough light to see a vehicle waiting, if there had been one. But there was no-one. Disappointed, she walked slowly home. She was so tired and, what was worse, she knew that she would be going back to an empty house. Ann was at Jim's cottage. It was only four days a week, but she missed her sister. Ann was the cook and home-maker. Eileen wished Martha had not invited her to stay. Of course it did make a difference in travelling; Ann had only ten minutes to walk to work, now that she was back at the nurseries. It pleased Jim, so that was more important. She didn't like leaving his mother alone in the cottage, especially as he was often working at nights now. Eileen worried about money too. The nurses and all the staff at the hospital would soon leave if they didn't get their pay. There had been no money since the invasion. First the banks closed down, with armed guards around them. Now they are open for an hour for Germans only. Rumours had it that they were changing the currency to their own but it was not substantiated.

She walked carefully, looking from left to right, scanning the corners and shop doorways, with fear in every step. It was not the Germans who put the terror in her heart, but her own people. They had waited for her friend Lily. When she finished work, neighbours pounced on her. A woman with scissors chopped off all her hair. Then they produced a tin of black treacle and poured it all over her face and neck. It was worse than tar, and all they could find to humiliate her.

Eileen could see the soldiers on guard at the end of her road. They were armed, but had their orders not to speak to women going home from work. It was a dangerous situation. Eileen's heart began to beat faster, making it thump in her breast. Terrified, she ran the last few steps to her door and put her key into the lock. Her hands trembled so much she could not turn it and then to her utter amazement, the gentle push had opened it. The door was already unlocked! Fumbling for the light switch, she put the passage light on, then the kitchen one.

'Ann!' she tried to call out but no sound came. Ann must be upstairs. What was she doing here? It was her time to be at Beech Cottage. Perhaps she herself had left the front door open herself this morning. Yes! That was it.

Calmer now, Eileen sat down for a second. It was then that she heard a soft noise in the front room. Mrs Sharpe's cat, she thought. I must have let him in this morning. She got up and took her coat off. She walked into the little front room, putting the light on as she did so.

'My God,' she gasped. There sitting in one of the leather armchairs, was Heinrich. He held out his arms for her to come to him, saying something in German that she didn't understand. She stood stiff and didn't move. When she spoke there was a confusion of tears and anger, spilling out. 'What do you think you are doing? Coming into my house, breaking in, sitting there? How dare you!'

He sprang to his feet, scaring her still further. 'No! No, fraulein, I did not break in. I rang the bell and then I saw the door was open, so I came in.'

She backed away from him as he went to touch her cheek with his hand. Her body was shaking. He moved closer.

'I am so sorry. Please do not be afraid of me. How could you think I would hurt you? I love you. Yes, yes, it is all right. I think you could love me too?'

She shuddered at the thought but he was not to be put off that easily. His mood was changing, there was force now in his arms as he lunged forward and gripped her by the wrists. With a quick jerking movement she managed to get away from him. Now they were playing cat and mouse and she was frightened. She kept walking away from him, putting the table between them.

'The answer to your question is no,' she said coldly.

'You will live to regret this.' There was a half-smile across his hard features. 'You see, Eileen, I always get what I want.'

Eileen still managed to keep the table between them. 'Get out! I want you out of my house.'

'Yes, I will go. I do not take what I want like an animal. I will find one instead who looks just like you.' He paused to let his words find their mark. 'It is not difficult, especially with, how do you say, identical twins. I will go for second best if I must.'

Eileen stopped dead and went stiff. She felt as if she had been beaten with a heavy stick. His cold steel eyes stared into hers as she screamed, 'No! Not Ann!'

Ethel was preparing her tea when she heard the screams. The girls were in trouble! Standing stock still she listened with growing alarm. What should she do?

Seconds passed, then minutes. The screams continued. She made up her mind. She would have to take the risk and go next door to their house. Maybe she would be attacked as well? But she felt she must go and find out.

With trembling hands she took the key from the dresser, made her way to the outside yard and put it into the back door of number seven. As she crept into the kitchen she noticed that the awful screaming had been replaced by the sound of sobbing. Eileen lay across the table, her head and face buried in her hands, crying uncontrollably. She was alone! Ethel let out a cry of relief at that and gathered Eileen up in her arms.

'There there, don't upset yourself like this darlin'. Did he hurt you?' Ethel held her tight, rocking her to and fro, stroking her hair.

It was some minutes before Eileen stopped crying. She lifted her head and looked lovingly at Ethel who had always been there for her when times had been bad, especially after Eileen's mother had died. She never needed her more than now.

'Thanks for coming round Ethel. He didn't touch me, it was what he said and what he is going to do that put the fear of God in me.'

Ethel led her gently to an armchair. 'Sit there my love. I'll make us a nice cup of tea and then you can tell me what happened. I saw that German officer come here, the one who gives you a lift to work.'

Ethel filled the kettle and put it on the gas ring. 'He got in through your kitchen window. You didn't put the catch across the top! I saw him and it made me so mad but what could I do? You either mind your own business and do nothing or get shot.'

As she came back to Eileen with a steaming hot mug of tea, she was drying her eyes with a tea cloth.

'We use very large hankies now, do we pet?' She grinned at Eileen, trying to make her laugh and the first smile appeared across her white face, up to her red-rimmed eyes.

'You are a real gem Ethel. Even better than a Ration Book full of coupons.' Then she began to tell Ethel all that had happened between herself and Heinrich, bursting into tears again at the thought of Ann.

'Look,' said Ethel. 'I had started to get tea for my family when I heard you screaming, love. I dropped everything and got here quick. Now I ought to get back to see to them. George still has a good appetite in spite of the rationing. I don't know how I make it go round, the ration for each of us is so small.'

She walked towards the door. 'I don't like leaving you like this. Perhaps I'll pop back later, my love.'

Getting to her feet, Eileen followed her to the outside door. 'Yes, please Ethel. I'm frightened to be here on my own now.' She gave Ethel a hug and watched her walk across the back yard to her own door. The light from her kitchen shining out across the yard made her suddenly remember the black-out and she quickly shut the door. Silly, she thought, there was no need for the black-out now as the Germans were unlikely to drop bombs on their own troops, yet everyone still kept the black cotton blinds up at their windows out of habit.

Eileen had regained her composure by the time Ethel returned later. The scraggy, warm-hearted neighbour cuddled her for a brief moment before sitting down by the fire with Eileen.

'You all right now dear?'

'Yes, thanks Ethel. I've had time to think things over and I've got a plan: I have to make sure he doesn't harm my sister. Ann is so vulnerable. She's sensitive and I promised mum I'd look after her.'

'Would he really hurt her?' asked Ethel.

'No. He wouldn't strike her but he could hurt her in other ways. He would force her to be his mistress! I must pretend to win him back and then use *him*. I've got some serious acting to do. The thought of it makes me sick but I must keep him away from Ann. If she gets in his clutches he will destroy her.'

'Yes, but what about you?'

'Me? Well, I'm a nurse; I've seen blood and had to battle with allsorts of horrors. I'm a lot harder than Ann. If I can see this through, you won't think any the less of me, will you Ethel? I'm not that kind of girl but some round here will think so if they see Heinrich coming into my house. And he will. It's blackmail!'

Ethel put an arm round her shoulder. 'Don't be silly. Of course I won't. I think you're very brave. If there's any gossip, I'll see that people are aware of your problem. Try not to worry. Do what you have to do.'

Giving her a wink, Eileen said, 'Do you know, it's so strange but I've a feeling that he won't be here long. Heinrich will be called to take more troops further up the country. That will be the last we shall see of him.'

'I hope you're right,' murmured Ethel.

Chapter 11

Ann felt strange to be back at the nurseries on her own. She missed the girls, especially Gwen, who made the day go quicker with her humour. Now she was not even on her old job with Joe. He had moved her to the flower shed, then a session in the packing shed. She loved packing the lovely bunches of early spring flowers, especially the golden daffodils. These were sent out on the early morning train to London before the invasion happened; now they went into Southampton.

Another pleasure was staying at Beech Cottage. She felt safe and happy with Jim's mother who she called 'Ma.' It was only ten minutes walk from work now, and she knew Wick Lane like the back of her hand. Only one thing intrigued her: The big house was so bleak-looking now, empty save for the owner of the nurseries. Cliff Dobbs apparently lived there on his own. Ann was sorry to hear from Joe the news that Cliff's wife had left him. She went by the house each morning to get to the nurseries and strangely enough, Ann could have sworn that she saw the upstairs curtains move slightly.

She and Joe worked late one night to get some plants in the ground. They worked with the low watt light on and when they had finished, Joe locked the greenhouses and looked for the boss to give him the keys. Not finding him, Joe decided to put the keys through the door of the house.

'Will you pop them in for me, Ann?' he asked brightly.

'Yes! Sure, Joe.' Ann got on well with Joe. They didn't see much of the boss. Cliff spent a lot of time with his hens. He had gone in for poultry more, even though it was so difficult getting corn for them. Joe reckoned Cliff talked to his hens.

She moved quietly across the turf to reach the house and was just about to push the bunch of keys through the letter box when she heard voices and laughter coming from inside. Under the impression that the boss was always alone in the big house, she was surprised and stood still for a moment. The voices were definitely German. They were conversing in their own language. She kept perfectly still. There were a lot of them. A hiss in her ear and Joe was standing beside her.

'Come on! Let's get out of here quick,' he whispered. They hurried away and, reaching the end of Wick Lane, Ann suddenly remembered that she was still clutching the bunch of keys.

'Joe! I'm so sorry!' She held them out for him to take.

'It's all right, Ann, don't upset yourself. I'm not going back with them now. Morning will do,' he said. 'Now let's get you to the Blake's cottage, see you safe home.'

The grass was crunchy under their feet.

'Frost!' he said.

'Will the new plants be all right?' she asked.

'Yes. Plants will survive.'

'No heating, you can't get the oil, can you, Joe?'

'No, but don't worry about that. They got hot-water bottles.' He chuckled and she knew by the dig in the ribs from his elbow that Joe was a leg-puller. They both giggled as he opened the wicket gate.

'There you are Miss, escort to your door.' The next minute he was gone.

Martha was at the door before Ann reached the step. She hugged her and led her into the cosy living room, where the fire was burning bright. It smelled sweet, not like the logs of wood at home.

'It's apple wood, you can smell,' Martha said, 'Jim chopped the tree down yesterday. The apples were nice, but the tree had a disease. It wasn't safe. We have to be careful with thatch, some wood is too dangerous, it sparks and pops.'

'I didn't know. We have slate tiles on our house.'

'Yes, now tell me how you're getting on. You like Joe, don't you? Jim and I have known the family for many years. He has a disabled wife, you know. But he never talks about her.'

'Oh! That is sad,' said Ann. 'He laughs a lot! You wouldn't know. We were asked to leave the keys at the house tonight. Well! Joe waited about for Mr Dobbs, but he never turned up, so we went to the house and heard voices, Germans. There seemed to be a lot of them. Anyhow, we got scared, so hurried away from the house. Joe said that we should leave the keys until the morning. They sounded like they were having a party. Funny! There were no cars or vehicles there.'

Martha had listened intently to what Ann was saying. There was a strange look on her face, as she said, 'I don't like the sound of this. Do you know what I think, Ann? Well, I would guarantee that it is a safe house. If things go wrong the top brass will use it for a bolt hole. They think because this is the New Forest it's safe. Hide here, no one will find them. Well, they don't know the Forest, do they? It's not all trees.'

She dished up the meat stew and she put a plateful in front of Ann.

'There, my love, you get that down you. Jim should be here any minute.'

He came home an hour later. His mother had kept his supper hot, and she fussed over him. Ann thought how tired he looked but he noticed her staring at him and his white face broke into a warm smile.

'How's the job going? Do you like it there at the nurseries?' he asked.

She nodded and then told him about her work and about Joe. When she got to the story about the keys, she noticed that he had stopped eating and had put his knife and fork down. Ann wasn't sure if he was worried or angry. He was certainly disturbed and got up from the table and walked into the kitchen.

'What's up with him?' his mother remarked as she picked up his plate. 'If the supper isn't hot enough, Jim, I'll re-heat some more stew.' She went into the kitchen, but he said crossly, 'Stop following me about Mum. I don't want any more. I just need peace!'

The two women looked at each other in surprise. Ann wondered if she was in the way. Should she be there at all?

134

'Is it me, Ma?' she asked. 'I'll go back home when I finish work tomorrow. It would be best.'

'No! Certainly not. You're here at my invitation, dear. I want you here for the four days a week that you work at the nurseries. And when you are out of a job I shall have you all day, all the week, so there. Jim is courting Eileen. You're my friend, so it's nothing to do with him.'

'Thank you, 'Ma, said Ann. 'That was a long speech. 'They both laughed, but tears welled up in her eyes. It was so nice to have a Mum to go home to. Ann had missed her beloved Mum.

After a while, Jim came back and sat in his chair by the fire. He motioned the two women to sit with him.

'We have to talk,' he said.' There are things I need to tell you. I can't carry it all alone. You have to know.'

Ann looked across at his mother, but she was looking at her only son, deeply. They could both tell that there was something seriously wrong, and his mother's feelings ran deeper than Ann's – or did they?

Jim told them of the changes in his work, but could not mention his involvement with the secret army. He hated the fact that he was leading a double life, keeping his activities a secret from his mother. The fact that operational units of the secret army were setting explosives along the railway tracks would have been worrying news for her. The day to day fear for his life would kill her. He did, however, tell both of them, because he trusted Ann, the information he had received on the Clifford Dobbs' large house. His mother did not know that his wife had left him, or that he now lived alone in one room there.

'I couldn't understand why I hadn't seen her lately,' his mother said. 'You know, Jim, how kind she was to us, bringing us tomatoes nearly every week.'

'Well! She's gone for good, Mum. It's sad.' Jim paused for a moment before he told her the bad news. 'The house is full of Germans, the officers and top brass. They live there. But they want to keep it a secret house – a bolt hole for them. Mum, they think no one knows they are there. In fact, they think the New Forest is a good hiding place.'

'Well! I'm sure they had a party on in the house when we left work tonight,' said Ann.

'We must keep quiet about it. It's our secret.' Jim was quite sure of their loyalty to him. 'One day soon our boys will blow it up, with all of them in it.'

The two women looked at Jim in horror.

'They wouldn't do that, would they? That house cost over eight hundred pounds to build, Cliff told me'.

'Stop, Mum. It's only bricks and mortar. We have to lead double lives now. We must pretend to be friends with the Germans, while we're making plans to get rid of them from our country. If needs must, then kill them.'

Jim's mother had not seen much of the invasion. The soldiers put on guard around the edge of the Forest had left the villages alone. They took food from the farmers and then left. They would appear and ask for eggs, sometimes a chicken from the cottages. It was a barter for a life. Poor Mrs Blake had referred to her callers at Beech Cottage as quite nice men, very polite for Germans. She had handed over the eggs and other items with a faint smile. She was not as silly as she looked because she had a cellar under the hen house. Eggs and food were stored, enough to last for months as it was very cold down there. She had bought some isinglass powder or crystals from the chemist months ago, and had put eggs in the bucket of liquid. It preserved them to last all through the winter.

It was a long evening. Jim kept the fire going with small logs of apple wood while they talked. He told them about the railway and the empty platforms, how all the trains out of Southampton had been stopped except for the two lines which were left for carrying troops, the line south as far as Lymington and his Southampton to Waterloo line that stopped at the German front line at Romsey. Then he told the two women there beside him of the horrors that were occurring every day: That several lines had been blown up, resulting in casualties; the biscuit factory, and a large, wholesale meat depot, all set on fire. By the owners! Unbelievable, but rather than let the enemy take it over, they destroyed it. Jim knew that there had been a contingent of Germans in a large hall, and the secret army had blown it up. There were no national newspapers getting through to the occupied area but an underground one with the loyal help of an editor and a printer, were producing a small daily paper with news of the city. People did not know what was happening around them. Two of the big hospitals were still going but so understaffed and short of drugs, that they were on the brink of disaster. Propaganda leaflets and posters were the only news at the moment.

'I'm under guard on my engine with a soldier on the footplate with me,' said Jim. 'I take a train load of German troops up to the front line most days.' Jim had to stop there. He could not tell them the entire story, how he wore the pin badge of 'rail workers' who worked for our own police force. Only today he had heard from the woman who gave him a message on the first day. She had followed him to the toilets at Southampton station and asked him to keep watch for two men. She showed him a photo of the men. 'They're Nazi scum. Here for trouble,' she said angrily. 'If you see them, blow your steam twice.'

Jim did not continue on that subject, or told Ann and his Mum that he had accomplished the task and the two men were captured at the gate, in front of their own soldier who was guarding the platform. He looked on the scene in innocence, seeing a couple of well dressed businessmen going off with two beautiful ladies. The fact they had guns in the sides, covered with the ladies' handbags, made it even more remote.

He knew neither his mum nor Ann would believe this piece of news, so he remained silent. Jim had started up the engine and had not seen her again until the return journey, which had seen the carriages empty except for some German casualties returning from the front line. The journey back had been uncomfortable and Jim had had to slow down at one junction as there were several railway linesmen at work on the line.

Jim had felt uneasy and tried not to think of the danger he was in. When he had been driving the engine up the line towards the fighting, he had felt real fear which stayed with him until he had returned to Southampton again. When he had left the station to go home, the woman had been waiting for him in a car and had called out to him. 'Get in for a minute,' she had whispered and Jim got in beside her.

'You did a good job today, quick off the mark. Of course, you know the women shot them both in the toilets. I locked it up and the cleaners have orders to dispose of the bodies,' she said coolly.

'What about the comeback? Will the cleaners talk?'

'No,' she said. 'Who is going to worry about two naked bodies? I stripped them. Now I've got a suitcase with Nazi clothes in to burn. Good day's work, Jim Blake.'

Jim got out of the car, but before he turned to walk away, she said softly, 'One to go! This one is Hitler's special man. Charming, too. He was sent to win over the Southampton population, until further orders.' She pulled up the car window and the next minute she was gone.

It was all still going round and round in his head. He knew now that the man she was looking for was here in Southampton.

He suddenly realised his mother was saying something to him and shook himself.

'Sorry Mum, I was deep in thought. What were you saying?'

'I asked if you have to drive that train. Couldn't you get another job?' she said it with a cross look on her face.

'If it was all that simple. By working for that officer, I am covered. We have an agreement; he looks after you, Ann, and Eileen, if I do.'

'I don't understand, Jim, but there, I won't say any more. I suppose it's what you trained for and like doing,' she said softly, not wishing to upset him.

Ann was the only one who really understood. Mrs Blake went out to the kitchen to make the bedtime drinks. It was then she heard the tapping on the back door. 'Whoever is that at ten o'clock at night?' she murmured to herself. Sliding back the bolts she opened the door. 'Oh It's you, Cliff,' she said, surprised to see the owner of the nurseries standing there. 'Can I help?'

'Yes,' he said, standing to one side to let the man behind him enter. 'This is Captain Shultz. He and his friends have come to supper with me. But all our lights are gone. Fuse or something. Have you got a few candles we can have to see the night out? We can repair it in the morning.'

Mrs Blake liked Cliff, so she said, 'Why, yes, of course. Come in by the fire while I find some for you.'

Heinrich stared at the two in the armchair. Ann had been kissing Jim's cheek and thanking him for looking after her and Eileen. She got up quickly out of the chair and went up the stairs before he had time to speak.

Jim got up and offered a box of matches to light the candles. He knew Heinrich so there was no need for introductions.

Cliff apologised for intruding on their evening and made some comment on the lovely fire, to which the German asked for some logs of the wood that burned so sweetly. Jim said that there was no more left, then meeting his cold stare he added, 'You're welcome to the other batch of logs stacked outside.' He even smiled as he said it but his hands were clenched so tightly behind his back that they hurt.

'I've not frightened Eileen away to her bed, have I?'

Jim did not correct him, but just said, 'She's tired. '

'She works hard,' the German said, with a slight sneer.

'She's been in the nurseries today.'

'Ach yes! The little ones!' Heinrich smiled at Mrs Blake as he said it. He took the box of candles and the matches. Cliff nudged him towards the door.

'Better go now. But thank you so much.'

'It's my pleasure to help if I can,' said Mrs Blake.'Goodnight Cliff. Goodnight Captain.'

Jim took them to the back door, and slid the bolt across when they were gone.

Mrs Blake and Ann went straight to bed. It had been a strange sort of day and both women were stressed out. Ann had taken an instant dislike to the German. So that was Eileen's so-called friend, she thought. Her first impression was not good. He had a cold, hard streak she decided. The she stopped to think. Well, Eileen was in a difficult position, and she had made it clear to Ann, that she was just using him. But it was Jim who held Ann's last thoughts before she went to sleep.

Jim did not go to bed for a long time. He sat the fire out and let his thoughts run riot around in his head. In the end he felt cold, so crept very softly up to bed. His bedroom was next to Ann's. As his head touched the soft pillow he thought of Ann. Sweet girl. Lovely nature. She thought a lot of his Mum. She was company for her, and he liked her company too.

As he drifted off to sleep, he heard the drone of heavy aircraft over his head, their dropping point not far away: Hundreds of paratroops were waiting to drop from the skies while he slept, ready to reinforce the German troops encircling Southampton and the New Forest and the front line which was pushing ever northwards towards the Thames and into the heartland of Britain.

Chapter 12

Eileen made out her time chart and signed off. It had been a sad and rather dreadful day on the Women's' Ward. Even Doctor Preston had moaned about the casualties, mostly women fighting each other, because of being accused of fraternising with the Germans. One woman had waited in a dark doorway with a wood chopper to attack her neighbour: She had sliced her like a butcher and had then waited to have a go at the poor woman's husband. Eileen and Matron had torn up sheets for bandages.

She put on her coat and made her way out of the hospital. There was the one and only taxi waiting for her. She got in as quickly as she could, afraid of angry faces always ready to hurt her. Heinrich was not there. The driver said his boss would be late.

Her house was dark and cold. As she lit the fire, she was surprised to see coal in the bucket. He must have brought it. Ann was still up at the Blake's' cottage, so it would not be her. Then she remembered that she had given Heinrich the spare key.

Mrs Sharpe came in as she was cooking her tea. Her eyes were sharp like her name. The first thing she asked Eileen was, 'Where did you get the coal?'

Eileen palmed her off with a lie. 'Jim Blake got me a little bagful when he stoked up his train.'

She accepted the answer, especially as Eileen added, 'I'll get him to wangle you a bit.'

Mrs Sharpe didn't stay long. Eileen was glad because she feared her next question would be, 'Where did you get your chops?' So she waited until she was gone before she put them in the pan. A glance at the clock and she waited for Heinrich to come in.

She rushed to him, excited when he did appear. He was a little bit cold towards her. For one thing he took off his jacket and sat in her chair. Funny, but she hated him doing that. It was her Mum's chair. He did not kiss her, that was another thing, but he asked her how work had been.

'I missed you yesterday and evening when you didn't come,' she said.

'I don't think you were lonely. He gave her a cool glance. You are still seeing Jim Blake.'

'No, I'm not!' Her voice rose. 'Something is biting you, Heinrich. Tell me what's wrong.'

He got up from the chair and towered over her. She was frightened but tried not to show it.

'Now you are mine! I asked you not to see him again. But you did. You were in the one armchair. Then you rushed out of the room and up the stairs when I came in the door.'

Eileen could not understand what he was talking about. She was baffled and he took her silence for guilt. It was a strange situation.

He described the scene at Beech Cottage, telling her about the candles and the logs. Suddenly, everything came into place and she laughed.

'Ah, you saw my sister, Ann, not me. We are identical twins. We do look so alike. She stays with Mrs Blake as a friend. It is only four days a week. That is nice because you and I have this place to ourselves.'

'I see,' he said calmly. 'So that was it.' He held her in his arms, a mixture of anger, passion and pride, clawing away at him. He kissed her passionately. With it all, he was not fully convinced, though.

'Did you nurse in the children's ward yesterday?'

'No! There are no children. They were all evacuated because of the bombing raids. They took bus loads to the country, for safety.'

He did not know whether to believe her or not. But his passion was like a tiger and he turned out the lights and carried her up the stairs to her bedroom.

'I can stay the night,' he whispered. 'But I must leave by seven-thirty in the morning. I have to go to Lyndhurst. I have ordered a meeting there with, how you say, verderers? The men who are the keepers of the New Forest. Their leader is to be present. He is called, I think, the Ajunster! No?'

'You're nearly right,' she whispered, as she buried her face in his neck. 'What about our meal I've cooked?'

'Don't talk, let us have tonight together.'

The following morning was anything but a honeymoon. The rain trickled down the bedroom window, and to make matters worse, they had over-slept. The bedside clock said seven o'clock. Eileen woke first. There was a panic. He was not very good tempered, blaming her for the situation. Both naked, it took them that few minutes more to dress.

His mood was a little frightening and she tried to help him by handing him his clothes, then he rushed down the stairs, complaining about her lack of bathroom. He certainly did not think much of the outside toilet.

Thank God he was going away to Lyndhurst. He may stay there for a while, he had said, much to her relief. Eileen could see his staff car out in the road. How did they know he would be here all night, she thought, or be here at all, come to that? He must have planned it and told his guard to pick him up in the morning.

There was no time for breakfast. Heinrich gave her a peck on the cheek and ran for the front door. It was not yet daylight, but she looked out of the door and watched him get in beside his driver. He said something to him and they both threw back their heads and laughed. Eileen closed the front door quickly and went back into the kitchen, her mind full of doubts.

She didn't stop for breakfast; there was not much time if she was going to Lyndhurst. Should she go or not? Heinrich had given in to her wishes last night.

'Please, take me!' she had pleaded and eventually, he had given in to her. But he had also warned her of the danger of being seen with him.

'You will have to walk behind me, not at my side,' he had told her. 'And you can not travel with me on the train. I will leave a rail pass at the station for you. You will not get on the train without it. We run that line for our men. Wear your nurse's uniform.'

'I didn't want to have to do that. It is my full day off, the first for weeks,' she moaned.

'Then don't come if you can't obey my wishes.'

He had turned over in bed and set his back to her. However, before sleep overtook him, he turned back and folded her in his arms. Love was there, adoration even but it was a selfish, domineering love. So long as she did what he ordered, it would last. Deep down inside she knew this too. She asked herself many times lately. Did he love her, or was she just useful to him?

As she was making the bed and tidying up the room, she still held the question in her mind. She went to the dressing table to brush her hair. It was then that she noticed Heinrich's gold wrist watch. He had left it behind in the rush to dress. She had not really seen it before, only on his wrist. Oh God! He would blame her for not reminding him. There was a white silk handkerchief also beside it, with his initials on. H.V.S.

It was a lovely watch: She picked it up and some tiny thread in the past made her study it more closely. Opening the back of the watch, her eyes caught sight of the names inside the cover. 'George, Fred, William – three brothers killed in First World War, 1914–1918.' They were inscribed very fine and neatly. Eileen stood there transfixed. It was all coming back now. Her hand shook so much, the watch danced and she had to put it down gently.

Little things started to return to her brain. Yes! She had seen this before. Eric Small was said to have a watch like this. These were his brothers. Bill Clarke had told her the story of the watch. How he had got the watchmaker to make a special face. It was all coming back. The fishermen who were pulled to safety when their fishing trawler capsized.

Her memory flashed back to fishermen in the hospital. One of them had had a watch like this under his pillow. Eileen could remember Doctor Preston telling her to put it back, that there were hundreds in the jewellers exactly the same. She had replaced it under his pillow, and she remembered his blue eyes. His hair was brown though, she remembered that too.

Of course, what a fool she had been, not to recognise those blue eyes. Maybe it was the gold rimmed spectacles he wore now. He had bleached his hair to blonde too.

By now Eileen was satisfied. In fact, she was sure beyond doubt. She picked up the watch again and taking it to the bedroom window, she pulled the curtains. Daylight flooded in and it had ceased raining. Looking at the face of the watch she could see the tiny little cross on the number eleven. Three little gold dots, one each on the cross for each brother. It was a work of art, so beautifully done, especially if you knew what to look for.

Leaving it on the dressing table for the time being, she wracked her brain to think how she was going to get it back to its rightful owner, Eric's widow. Eileen's head was in turmoil. How could she think of him as a killer? Not after last night and yet the vision of the watch flashed across her eyes, as they filled with hot tears. She got ready for the train journey to Lyndhurst, no longer feeling the freedom of a rare day off work.

She hurried to lock the front door and then, just in case he came back to the house, she locked it with the bolt, and left by the back door, as only she and Mrs Sharpe had a key to that.

Her dislike of him filled her with horror. How could she keep up this pretence? It would have to stop. Ann would have to be protected in other ways.

Good job the train was late going, or she would not have made it. Her pass to board was there, but there was no sign of Heinrich. Eileen found a seat between two men in grey suits. They never spoke, or answered her friendly, 'Good morning.' No sign of Jim Blake, perhaps that was why the train was fifteen minutes late.

She got out of the carriage and looked up the platform to the engine. Jim had not turned up and she could see that they were getting another driver. When she got back in the carriage, she found that some more people had got in, so it was a squeeze to perch between two more passengers. It was then she saw him. Heinrich had got in the next carriage. He had two officers with him, and there was some heel clicking when the last one got into the carriage.

Eileen suddenly felt tired and battled with her eyelids to stay up but sleep overtook her. She dreamed of summer days and her mother loaded up with a hamper for a picnic, Ann pulling her hair and eating the last fish paste filled sandwich. It was lovely lying on the grass in the park with her head on Mum's lap.

'Come and have a game with the ball,' her sister kept wailing. Then there was a bang and she could not remember any more. It went all black.

Chapter 13

Jim was up first that morning. He made a big pot of tea and took his mother up a cup. He was a bit shy about taking Ann some tea but he was saved the embarrassment by her appearance on the stairs, dressed ready for work.

'Good, you've made the tea,' she said.

'Did you sleep well?' he asked.

'Yes!' she answered. 'I felt warm and safe.' Beech Cottage has that effect on people

'I'm so glad you're here if only for four days a week. Mum has looked better since you came. I know she's a bit scared of the Germans, yet they treat her kindly Ann. She put on a good face for that one last night, didn't she?'

It was the first time she had set eyes on Eileen's so called friend. Her sister did keep a bit from her, but she knew they were having an affair. She could tell he had been to the house. Another thing she disliked was Eileen's cooling off with Jim. She had made so many excuses not to see him. Martha had noticed it.

'You're quiet,' Ann, said Jim over breakfast. 'Penny for your thoughts.'

'Oh, they're not worth a penny.' She ate her toast, waited for Jim's mother to come down then she went off to work. It was only ten minutes' walk to the nurseries so Jim went with her as he felt that it was not really safe on her own. Then he went on to work himself.

The journey into Southampton took Jim over half an hour on his bike but that was because the German patrols had stopped him. His anger had raged within him but he had remained calm on the outside. They had been polite and were getting to recognise him.

When he reached Central Station the station master was waiting for him and handed Jim a timesheet.

'An officer left this for you.'

Jim's face changed. 'Lyndhurst!' he snapped. 'We have been doing Romsey every day, taking reinforcements to the front line.'

The Station Master shrugged his thin shoulders.

Just at that moment Jim saw his old Home Guard mate, Ray Wicks, approaching.

'How did you get past the guards? What are you doing here?'

'Got a pass card,' said Ray. 'I've got bad news Jim. It's your mum. I've just left her on the kitchen floor, unconscious. You must come back now to Beech Cottage with me. She needs you Jim!'

'She was all right when I left home,' muttered Jim, in shock.

Ray Wicks glared at his old mate in annoyance. 'Come on Jim. I've got the van, let's go! Take your bike and put it in the back of the van.'

The Station Master nodded his head. 'Go on. I'll get another driver.'

Jim was impressed by his calmness. He himself was very edgy. With a quick move, he ran out of the station, eager to get to his mother, praying all the time that she would be all right.

It was a nightmare journey. He flung open the gate and let himself into the cottage. Ray Wicks threw his bike on the grass and followed him indoors.

'Mum! Where are you?' His voice was filled with love and fear.

'Here,' she said, 'whatever have you come back for?' She was sitting in her chair with some sewing on her lap.

Ray Wicks looked rather uncomfortable. He shifted from foot to foot. Then he said, 'Well, my wife sent me down here with some scones she made. I had to give some to you. But, Martha, you were flat on the floor. I looked through the window. I got on my bike and went to get Jim. Bit impulsive of me. I should have gone back for my wife. How did you manage to get up?'

'Easy, Ray. I often drop my thimble, only this time it rolled right under the dresser. I had to lie down flat and get it out with a long knitting needle.'

White faced and speechless, Jim sat in the kitchen and put his head in his hands. The world was upside down. So many little things changing his way of life. Eileen had just dropped him. It was weeks now since they had spent some time together. She had cooled off and was spending time with this German Captain. People had seen them together going into her house.

Suddenly he felt his Mum beside him. She gently took his hands from his face, pretending not to see the tears sliding down his face. She kissed the top of his head and said softly, 'Shall we have a cup of tea, love? Ray Wicks is a nice chap.

He is so caring, especially to you. He puts his own head on the line for you sometimes, you will know one day.'

Jim felt the words burn into his brain ... 'on the line for you.' Of course! The truth hit Jim like a thunderbolt. Ray and his unit had been busy all night, setting the explosives up at the line. The train was going down with a load of top Germans on board. He should have been driving that train! Ray couldn't warn him before so he had made up that story about Jim's mother being in need of help. Clever! The train had left Southampton at five past eight with the relief driver on board, probably the German soldier, as the station master had said. And Bob Stack the fireman. Jim knew he had seen him.

Sadness nearly overwhelmed Jim. Bob was only eighteen. Jim let the tears come and he felt a sudden hatred for the Germans.

Jim noticed Ray picking up his bicycle to leave and ran outside to catch him. 'Wait, Ray! Thanks.'

Ray stopped and looked hard at Jim. His voice was no more than a whisper as he said, 'Forget it. I've saved your life but put my own at risk: The lads in my unit would kill me for releasing information. We all swore an oath of secrecy. Tell your mother to stay up in her bedroom and pretend to be ill, if only for today. She may have visitors!' He rode off into the Forest and Jim went back into the cottage. He knew that the Secret Army had put plastic explosives under the line and the train had crashes, and possibly been blown up. And he was supposed to have been on that train!

Martha brought him a cup of tea. 'Here you are son. You're so lucky.'

'In what way, Mum?'

'I can't tell you that. The war has brought a lot of suffering but the invasion has brought a lot of people together even more deeply than in peace time. There are good people out there.'

Jim looked at his Mother. She knew a lot more of what was going on than he gave her credit for. She was stronger than he thought too. Inner strength. He took the cup of tea she offered and gave her a warm smile.

'I'm not going back,' he said. 'We'll spend a bit of time together for a change. I'm never here.'

'Yes! That's good. We'll have our Ann this evening for company. She is nice to have around.'

He didn't answer, but he winked his eye, and the half smile expanded to a grin.

When Jim got to the station the next morning, the station master grabbed him by the sleeve and pulled him into his office, closing the door and locking it.

'Sit down,' he said.

'What's up?' said Jim, feeling that there was no time to sit. He had his engine to prepare for the day's journey.

'You won't be going anywhere, Jim. You have no train. Someone laid explosives under the track through the Forest yesterday, near Lyndhurst. The whole lot was derailed with dreadful results. I've heard early this morning one or two carriages were blown to bits. Didn't you hear the explosion from your house?'

154

'No. What about the people who were on it?' asked Jim, feeling sick.

'As you know, Jim, they had to hand their passes to me so I would say it was all Germans. One woman, she was a nurse, had her uniform on.'

'No! Was she with a German, an officer?' Jim muttered. 'It couldn't be Eileen.'

'No! But the officer, a Captain Shultz was on the train. There were some high-ranking officers got on at the last moment.'

'Oh my God! Who was the driver?'

'He was the German replacement. He was on the railway at Stuttgart before he joined Hitler's army. No loss to us, Jim, a German. But he's a human being. It all happened about mid-morning, yesterday but we only heard details this morning.'

'The nurse, you didn't know her, I suppose?' asked Jim.

'Well, no. She was just a nurse and on her own. One of the Germans brought her pass in earlier. How is your mum?' He was looking at some papers on his desk and didn't look up. 'Is she all right now after the fall?' He sounded so casual, especially as Jim's mother knew the family well.

'Yes. She's all right now.' Jim didn't say any more. He felt a little embarrassed, and at the same time he was uneasy about the change of drivers. There was just something not quite right about it. Ray Wicks had let it slip only a few days ago, that our boys were putting explosives on the track, under the rails. Ray had made him promise on honour that he would never repeat the conversation they had that night.

The station master broke into his thoughts. 'Are you all right? You do look white.'

'I feel rotten,' said Jim. 'It's been a shock. I have to find out who the nurse was? You know that I was courting a young nurse from Southampton hospital, did you?'

The other man shook his head. He had heard rumours about Nurse Smith, but he knew better than to talk.

'I'm going to the hospital to find out,' said Jim.

'I don't advise that,' said the station master. 'If I were you I'd lay low for a few days. Someone may ask why you weren't driving that train. I should go home and stay there.'

Jim thought for a moment then he left the station.

He did go straight home but he was a worried man. His mother looked surprised to see him again.

'There's no work,' he said wearily, 'so I'm not getting paid. Good job I got some savings.' He had to tell his mother about the train disaster as she obviously didn't know. There were no newspapers since the invasion and no telephones so it was a bit isolated here in the Forest. As soon as they had enjoyed their cup of tea together, he sat quietly holding Mum's hand and told her all there was to know about the explosion. He waited a while before he mentioned Eileen. As he said, there was no proof that it was her. They would have to find out if she had told another nurse that she was going to Lyndhurst. Jim emphasised how unlikely it was, and his Mum agreed.

The next thing was he had to voice his fears to Ann when she came home from the nurseries. This was the worst task he had ever had to do but he had to tell her. Jim and his

156

mother sat quietly contemplating how they could find out any news.

'What about a taxi? You could go to the house, you have a key.'

'No Mother, Eileen asked for it back,' he said.

'Well, what about going straight to the hospital and asking to see her?' His mother was trying all areas of thought.

'Another thing, Mum, you can't order a taxi now. The Germans took all the cars for their own use.'

'Well go and ask Mr Webb, he let you borrow his van once.'

'It's the petrol, Mum. He had run out, last time I asked.'

'Well, go across to the farm and ask him. Did you ever put that bolt on his door for him?'

'No. He asked me a week ago. I forgot.' Jim put on his raincoat and pulled up the collar. He was gone before Mrs Blake could say any more.

He was in luck. Bill had managed to obtain a can of petrol for his tractor and he urged Jim to go ahead and find some news in town. 'Do the bolt on the door tomorrow, Jim,' he said coolly. 'First things first. Take the van. You're welcome to it.'

When Jim reached Southampton, he drove straight to the hospital. It was so busy with casualties that it made Jim feel ill to see them but Matron saw him and took him back to her office to talk.

The first question she asked Jim was, 'Where's Eileen? She hasn't been to work for three days, one of which had been her first and only day off. She should have done the late night shift, also the early one at six-thirty this morning.'

Jim felt a stab of fear, as he explained about the rail disaster, which Matron had already had news of through the Red Cross. She brushed aside his concern and the suggestion that Eileen might have been on the train that had blown up. 'No Mr Blake, you're on the wrong track. She wouldn't go to Lyndhurst on her own, without you.'

He smiled and thanked her for her time.

'We need Eileen, Nurse Smith here now,' she said. 'These casualties coming in are from the Baker's shop in Onslow Road. There was some fighting in the queue over a loaf of bread and some young soldiers got nervous and opened fire on them. All the beds are full now, we need our nurses,' said Matron.

Jim left the hospital and decided to head for Granmere Road. Eileen could be there all the time. No longer having a key now, he knocked on the door and waited. The thing that most concerned him was that the curtains top and bottom were still across and he couldn't see through the parlour window. Then he went around the back and knocked the scullery door. The curtains at the back of the house were still across too. He was on the point of leaving when a woman's voice behind him said, 'What do you want?'

It was Mrs Sharpe and as he turned to face her, she cried, 'Oh! It's Mr Blake, I think, isn't it?'

'Yes! We have met once. You're Mrs Sharpe if I remember. I've called to see if she's home. We haven't seen her for a few days,' he said, with a worried frown.

'No. I haven't either. I think she must have gone away, because there have been no lights on at all. Ann's not there, either.'

'No, well, Ann's all right, you see she's staying with Mum. Ann works at Wick Lane Nurseries now. It's near our cottage in the Forest. She stays the four days a week she works. Company for Mum, too. Eileen agreed to the idea because of transport.'

Mrs Sharpe looked relieved. 'I'm glad Ann is with you.'

'She is due back here tomorrow; you'll see her, Mrs Sharpe. She'll tell you all about the nurseries. Ann says she likes it there. She and my mother are great friends.' He turned to go. There was no more he could do here. He wanted to get Bill's van back and was nervous about parking it in the street for too long.

Back in the Forest he put the van in Bill's old barn and walked back across the fields to Beech Cottage. He really had not felt like talking to Bill, at least now now. He decided to tell him the news in the morning when he went over to fix the bolt on their kitchen door.

He put his hand up and stopped his mother asking a lot of questions when he got in. 'Later!' he said. 'And, no. Mum, Eileen is nowhere to be seen. I begin to think she was on that train.'

'Oh Jim! I hope you are wrong. She's a lovely girl. What are we going to tell Ann?'

Ann went back to Southampton the next day. She had taken the news a lot more calmly than they had expected, and insisted on sleeping in her house, unafraid.

Mrs Sharpe came into the kitchen with a hot meal for her at midday. She offered to sleep in the house with her, but Ann insisted she was all right.

Jim missed Ann, so did his mother. He was also worried about her and decided to go to Southampton to see her. When he got to number seven he noticed the difference. The curtains were drawn back and the house looked less gloomy. Ann had found that being busy had helped, so she had cleaned the place from top to bottom. He offered to help and cleaned the old stove in the kitchen, then lit the fire. The house was very cold after Beech Cottage.

Ann showed him what she had discovered upstairs. 'Look what I found on Eileen's dressing table,' she said, 'It's a man's watch, gold, and there was this rather nice silk handkerchief with it. It has initials in the corner – HVS.'

Jim took it from her and opened up the back of the watch where he could see three names. 'It's not a German's watch Ann,' he said slowly.' The name William is English. If it was German, it would probably have been spelt Wilhelm. Keep it safe; don't let anyone see it until we've had a word with the police.

'No, You look after it Jim, until she comes back. She must have had a man in her bedroom.' Ann couldn't understand. Why would she sleep with anyone else but Jim? She had thought that they were in love. She looked at Jim sadly with tears in her eyes. 'How could she?' she whispered.

'Don't worry,' he said, 'she had been cooling off for some time. I felt she didn't want me.' He felt sad. There were still so many things he could not tell Ann. He put the watch and handkerchief in his coat pocket. He knew what had happened. Heinrich Shultz had slept with Eileen and in the morning he had taken her to Lyndhurst with him. That meant they were both gone. The horror of it all sent his mind reeling. He would have been killed too, if it had not been for his old mate and neighbour, Ray Wicks. Had Ray really seen his mother on the floor that day? There was something funny about the whole thing. For one thing, his mum could never have got to her feet on her own, he knew. Memory of an incident a few weeks ago when she fell flat on the sitting room carpet. She had shouted for ages before he came from the woodshed and saw her lying there. He remembered how he had pulled her up and she had joked about growing old and fragile.

Ann said suddenly, 'Are you all right Jim?'

'Yes! Fine.' He realised he was standing staring into space and pulling himself together, he did a few more jobs for Ann before he left. He got some more coal in from outside and dry wood.

'I should go now Jim,' Ann said as she pulled the front room curtains apart. 'Hurry! There are two soldiers outside looking at Mr Webb's van. Did you borrow it again?'

'Yes! Right, I'm off. Be careful Ann.'

It was not easy trying to explain to the German soldiers that he only had enough petrol to get back home. He did not have a spare can that they could seize so eventually they let him go, and he felt uncomfortable seeing that they were armed. The dwindling supply of petrol in the port was serious.

Mrs Sharpe came in to see Ann again in the afternoon. She was on her mettle about something and Ann noticed her sarcasm. It was over the bucket of coal, quite unaware of its origin, Ann said innocently to their neighbour, 'Yes! Eileen must have twisted someone's arm to get this. Jim Blake, I dare say. He has access to fuel.'

The deep frown from Mrs Sharpe's face suddenly lifted, and when Ann said, 'We'll share it with you,' she changed completely.

'Is that someone at your front door, Ann?'

'I'll go and see.' Ann opened the front door and Doctor Shaw from the hospital was standing on the step.

'Good gracious! I've not seen you for a long time,' Ann murmured shyly. 'Come inside, Doctor.'

He was no stranger. He had often called to take Eileen out for an evening.

Ann took him into the kitchen and introduced him to Mrs Sharpe, who, like a frightened bird, quickly made her exit.

'Eileen's not here,' Ann said, calmly. 'We are expecting her back, of course.'

Doctor Shaw looked deeply at the lovely girl facing him. 'You don't think she was a victim of the rail smash?' he said, staring hard at her.

'No! Of course not. We're identical twins, you know. I would know if her life had ended. We have a strong bond between us.'

'That's good. May I sit down?' His hand was shaking, as he pulled a kitchen chair forward.

'Yes, of course Doctor. Will you have a cup of tea with me?'

'Yes, please, that would be nice,' he said, the emotion of the moment doing something to his voice. He decided he would wait until she had her cup of tea before breaking the news to her. The likeness between the two girls was outstanding. In fact, if you did not know that there were two, you would have easily mistaken her for Eileen.

She poured out the tea and sat down opposite him. 'Now, John, that is what my sister referred to you as, John, you have not come here for nothing. What was it you came to tell me?'

He looked deeply into her eyes. 'I have come to tell you that Eileen is in a bed in the hospital, under my care. She is alive, but badly wounded. I'm unable to tell you in detail. It is best you come into the hospital and Matron and Sister will explain the injuries, which are serious.'

'How I'd love to see her,' said Ann, softly.

'She won't know you, Ann. Your sister is in a state of trauma. At the moment she is drifting in and out of consciousness. We are doing everything to help her.'

Tears slid down Ann's cheeks, but she never made a sound. Then, after a while, the questions flowed. 'How did she get back here, John?'

'Well, now, it was our Red Cross who rang the hospitals to find out where she worked. She did have her nurse's uniform on. There was a lot of trouble on the site as it was a train load of Germans. Very top rank. In fact, it was said about ten of them were Hitler's top men here to run things on a German state. They were all killed. The only survivors of the explosion were Eileen, a small boy of about seven, and the guard in charge of the last truck, the guard's van. He has worked on the railways for thirty years. There was one other woman, but she died after being pulled from the wreckage. She was thought to have been an undercover agent. Also an old man with a beard was among the dead bodies found in the wreckage: He was a German spy in disguise. Rescue workers noticed his youthful hands on such an old man. They stripped the blood-stained clothing off him and discovered a young body covered with a clever disguise, plus a German tattoo on his upper arm.'

'Good gracious, John! Where did you get all this information from?'

'The Red Cross, and our police, plain clothes police,' he said.

'Can we go now and see my sister?'

'Yes, Ann, but they won't let you stay long. Oh, and prepare yourself because she does not look good. You must be brave. She has internal injuries and she will never be able to have children. That is, if she lives. It's in the balance.'

Chapter 14

Jim Blake pushed his food around the plate while his mother watched, knowing that he was hurting. Eileen had been his woman; he made excuses for her lately and tried to believe that he still held her love.

'Don't eat it if you don't feel hungry.'

'Sorry, Mum, you cooked it so nice too. She's gone! I must get on with life, and not look back. It's all so sad though, Mum. Do you miss Ann being around?' he said quietly.

'Yes!' Mrs Blake sighed. 'You know, son, I've grown to love her, she is so uncomplaining, lovely nature. I suppose you won't mind if I ask her to keep the four days going?'

'Well, Mum, she may want to stay in her own home. Don't push it.'

'No, I would not do anything you didn't want.

There was a tap at the door and Jim wondered who was calling at this time of day. His mother opened the front door and let Ray into the sitting room. Jim opened his eyes and greeted his old mate. 'Anything wrong?'

'No,' said Ray, 'I just wanted to warn you, that's all.'

'Of what?' asked Jim.

'To advise you not to go anywhere near the station. It may be dangerous to be seen, as you are the train driver who was not driving the fateful engine that day. Also, Jim, they will be bringing back the remains. The whole station will be guarded.'

'Thanks for the warning Ray. What did the station master say? You have prepared him?'

'Yes, he knew. These Germans here are in deep trouble with Hitler. The invasion has not been going according to Hitler's plans. The word is, Hitler has not enough soldiers to send any more. It was a small invasion force sent to our port of Southampton to capture and hold it. It was intended to be the disembarkation point for the main assault but they hadn't bargained for the RAF still in control of the skies over the Channel and our navy lads keeping them from crossing with the main invasion force. We also know they're confident that no one will be able to defeat them on land. Do you know, Jim, they actually believe we have no army now, since Dunkirk. The ragged, beaten army that swam back had no guns, clothing or boats, to fight on.'

'How do you know all this, Ray?'

'Well, I got round one of the soldiers and made friends with him to suit my purpose, of course. He speaks good English. He tells me a lot of what's going on among them. I tell him a nice load of rubbish. So I got to know they are clearing the line and bringing home the remains of their own. They have lost a lot of their men lately. Did you know last night there was another big hall that went up? Someone had laid explosive in there, just as a big group of Germans were billeted inside. That was thirty more killed.'

'Who keeps laying these explosives?' asked Jim.

Ray looked long and hard at him, and then said, 'Secret Army. Telling them they're not wanted and eventually our regular troops will get themselves organised and re-equipped and come down from all over the country and free us. You'll get warning about when to stay locked in your homes. There will be no bombs, tanks, armoured cars. It'll be hand to hand fighting.

Now I must go, Jim but before I do,

I must tell you I heard something odd. They brought the nurse who was on the train back. She's in Southampton hospital. Being English the Red Cross found her and took over. The German troops wouldn't let them touch their bodies. In fact they turned the Red Cross away by force.'

'Oh my God! Is it Eileen, Nurse Smith? Did they say her name, Ray?'

'No, Jim, that's all I know, and that is very little.'

'Is she alive?' Jim looked devastated.

'Look, Jim, I can't tell you. My conversation with the informant was hurried and whispered in my ear. I couldn't ask questions.'

'I'll go to the hospital tomorrow,' said Jim. 'I've got to find out.' He looked at Ray. 'I'll keep my head down and won't go near the station.' Ray gave him a strange look.

'Now, I must go.' Ray started to walk to the door. Jim's mum, who had been in the kitchen, appeared suddenly. 'Good to see you, Ray,' as she opened the door for him. 'Bye.' She winked her eye and he grinned. Then he was gone.

The following morning there was another explosion. This time a large hotel opposite the Southampton railway station had been targeted. Like the rail explosion, it was the Secret Army's way of saying, 'You're not welcome.' There were approximately one hundred German military billeted there. Only two days before, they had taken over the Class A hotel.

167

The only English residents were the owners, an elderly couple who had been given the chance to go out: A lot of risky organisation had gone into saving their lives. They had received an invitation from the brewery to attend a buffet lunch at the Civic Centre at 12 p.m. that fateful day.

Jim Blake left Beech Cottage about eleven o'clock and went straight to the hospital. He heard the explosion at the railway station but, as he headed for the ward and little bed where Eileen lay, nothing else seemed to matter. The sister took him to see her, allowing him just ten minutes.

'No talking,' she said, pulling aside the curtains from around the bed.

The shock of seeing what had been such a beautiful girl, now this frail, battered body, was almost too much to bear. With tears running down his face, he bent over to touch her cheek. She opened her eyes and stared up at him.

'Jim,' she whispered, and then she closed her eyes again but not before the tiniest smile swept rapidly across her face. It was there and then it was gone. He bent down even lower and gently brushed his lips against her cheek.

'I love you. I'll take care of you,' he said softly. There was no movement, not a flicker, and she lay still now.

The sudden movement behind him and the soft swish of the curtain shattered the silence.

'Good afternoon, Mr Blake.' It was Doctor Shaw. He motioned Jim to join him outside and gently pulled back the curtain. 'You do know she is very ill. She had three fractures, legs, right arm and shoulder. Lucky her face only suffered a little bruising, but her right leg was crushed. But, Mr Blake, she is alive and fighting.'

Jim felt tongue-tied; he did not know what to say. Then he looked at the doctor and remembered that the doctor had taken Eileen out.

'She spoke! She said 'Jim!'' he said, triumphantly.

The expression on the doctor's face was like a marble statue as he shook his head. 'A few more days she will, Mr Blake,' he muttered as he moved away. Then he turned his head, 'And Matron wishes to see you.'

Matron did not have a lot of time to spare. She sat with Jim Blake and talked of her Nurse Smith. Eileen was one of her best nurses. She did her best to explain Eileen's present condition. Her face lightened when she said how dedicated Doctor Shaw was, to Nurse Smith.

'He hardly leaves her side, you know. There is never a night that he isn't there, sitting by her bed. I had to have a go at him about lack of sleep. We have other patients on the wards that need attention. Well, Mr Blake, do feel free to come and talk to me if you are worried about her any time. She has still a long way to go. But I know she will make it.'

Jim smiled at her as he said with pride, 'Eileen spoke to me. "Jim!" she said. Nothing else. She opened her eyes and looked straight at me, and then she smiled.'

Matron put her hand across the desk and put it on Jim's. 'That's wonderful. Doctor Shaw has not had that privilege. Nurse Smith didn't give her smiles away to anyone on legs.'

Jim got up to leave. 'Thank you, Matron, I will visit again tomorrow.'

When he got home to Beech Cottage, Jim's mother was sewing. She was sitting by the open fire and watched as her son slumped into his armchair. He was silent. She concentrated on her sewing and left him to make the first move. Fear knotted her stomach as she began to wonder what happened at the hospital. Was Eileen dead or was it someone else's body? The clock ticked away the time, and the fire burned low.

'Ready for your supper, Jim?'

'Yes, please. Sorry, Mum. I've had a lot of things on my mind. After supper we'll talk. Eileen is alive, but critically ill.'

'Bless her, poor girl. Will you make a pot of tea while I dish up the rabbit pie?'

'Yes, sure Mum. I don't know what I would do without you! Today has been an awful day.'

'We get a few of those in our lives, all of us, Jim. Most of us survive because we have to.'

Ann was looking forward to going back to work. It was lonely in the house all day. Mrs Sharpe was good to her, but she had worries of her own. Her son, George, was out of work and had been seen hanging around the old Empire Theatre. This was a notable gambling place and occasionally a lot of money exchanged hands. The managers had no say in the matter since the Germans took over the place.

Ann had visited the hospital every day and had seen very little progress in her sister's condition. The only consolation was that her sister Eileen now said a few words to her. It was also nice to meet Jim on the same visit. He came back with her once and they had made a cup of tea and talked together.

'You really still love my sister, don't you, Jim?'

'Yes,' he said softly.

Ann had clenched her fingers, digging her nails hard into the palms of her hands and said to him sharply, 'After all she has done to hurt you!'

He had turned away and had made no answer, making her wish she had kept her mouth shut. Couldn't he see what was starting to grow right under his own eyes? Her sister only had eyes for Doctor Shaw.

It was Ann's day to go back to work, so she made her way to the Bargate and waited for Cliff Dobbs' van. She was surprised to see Gwen Bailey waiting too.

'Hello, Ann!'

'Hello, Gwen. Are you back at the nurseries?'

'Yes. I had a message to say come back for a couple of days a week.'

'I only do four,' said Ann. 'Cliff hasn't got the money to pay people longer hours. I have missed you, Gwen.'

The van appeared as she said that, so they got in quickly and rode off through the Forest to Wick Lane, and the nurseries.

Cliff was in his office and came out to show them what it was he needed them to do. A new officer had arrived to see him and was making a standing order for flowers every day. At least thirty large bunches. Cliff spoke straight to the officer and told him firmly that he demanded payment for all flowers. No more free ones.

'What do you mean, Mr Dobbs?'

He averted his eyes from the gun in the holster, stood pole straight and looked the German in the face. 'Sir, I have never received one coin for all the flowers and pot plants your men have taken. I've no money to pay my workers,' he said.

'You are the owner, or manager of this business?'

'I am the owner.'

'Then I shall see that you are paid, and recompensed for the free ones.' He made a stiff salute, clicked his heels and disappeared out into Wick Lane where a car was waiting with three guards sitting in the back, all armed.

The two girls had made a quick exit to the potting shed when they saw the German officer coming through the gates.

'Armed men can be very intimidating,' Ann whispered to Gwen.

As soon as he was gone, Cliff came across to the girls. 'Good news. They are real paying customers. I shall soon be in a position to take you on full time.'

When the girls left work at five o'clock, Gwen was the only one going back to Southampton in the van.

'Aren't you coming?' she asked.

'No. I've had an invitation to stay here in Beech Cottage. It's only ten minutes' walk from here,' said Ann.

'You lucky thing!' Gwen laughed, as she hoisted her plump body up into the van. Joe got in and they drove off.

Ann let herself in through the back door of Beech Cottage to find that Jim and his mother were in the kitchen.

'It's so good to see you, Ann,' said Martha, taking her hand. 'I hope you're hungry?'

'Yes, I'm starving.' Ann kissed her cheek and she shyly looked across at Jim. He smiled and patted her shoulder.

'Been to the hospital today to see Eileen,' he said. 'You know, Ann, she is getting better. She spoke my name. I went in to Matron before I left, and had a few words with her. She said the same; she is improving just that little bit each day.'

Martha stood stock still for a moment, staring straight ahead. 'She will pull through then,' she whispered. It was as if she were talking to herself. Her face was pale with lack of expression.

After their meal, they sat together around the table for a long time, talking. The conversation broached many subjects, but finally settled around the gold watch still inside Jim's coat pocket. Unknown to Ann, he had made a few enquiries about it and his efforts had not been in vain, as Ray Wicks had made contact with Bill Clarke. Ray was Eric Small's mate and had waited to take revenge for his death. He was the only one who could actually identify the watch. If he could prove it was the property of Eric, Jim could go ahead and give it to the widow, Daisy Small, who should have it. He would have to be careful. Once the Germans heard of it, they would claim it as Heinz Schultz's. He had been a popular officer among his own men when he was alive.

All these thoughts whirled round in Jim's head. Finally, he said, 'Mum do you mind if I bring Bill Clarke back here for a chat?'

'Of course I don't, Jim.'

The next few days were very strange and Jim could not contact any of the Home Guard. Bill Clarke's wife told Jim that she had not seen him for three days.

'Worried? Of course I am,' she told him. 'I don't let myself think of the possibilities.'

Jim went to see Ray and there he was met with the same answers, as his wife had not seen him for three days. The mystery continued and Jim felt a deep sense of fear.

Eileen was making a remarkable recovery and she was now able to sit out in a chair. Though still painfully thin, she had colour in her skin and talked more, remembering the past. She asked after their little house and said that she longed to go back there and sit once again in her late Mum's chair.

One day she asked Jim about the watch. When he told her that he had it for safe keeping, she set her mouth in a thin line and reminded him that it belonged to her.

'It was Heinrich's,' she said, sharply. 'I shall return it when he comes back.'

'But he's not coming ...' Jim started to say but he saw Matron put her hand up, and had to stop.

'Hasn't anyone told her?' Jim whispered to Matron.

She shrugged her shoulders. 'We only give out good news or sad. He does not come under either.'

When Jim arrived to see her the following week, she was just being gently lifted out of bed by Doctor Shaw. They had not noticed him so he drew back at the side of one of the curtains. Doctor Shaw held her close for quite a while, and then he lowered his head and kissed her. It was hardly the kiss of a friend, and Jim looked sadly on the little scene played out in front of him. He knew it was over. She was not going to be part of his life, his future.

He turned quietly to go, but unfortunately Matron was at his elbow. 'It's good to see her out in the chair, Mr Blake, isn't it?'

Eileen looked up over Doctor Shaw's shoulder, as he was tucking a rug around her legs in the chair.

'Hello, Jim. Fancy seeing you. Are you all right?'

'Yes! Fine,' said Jim hiding the knowledge behind a broad smile.

'How's Ma?'

'Mum's all right, and Ann. They send their love and will be in on Sunday to see you,' he said. He looked at Eileen, but she was gazing up at the face of Doctor Shaw, who seemed reluctant to leave her. Jim turned to go, and said goodbye, but she hadn't heard him so he slipped quietly out of the hospital. He would not go again.

Ann was the only one to visit her sister. When she came back, she told Jim that Eileen and John Shaw were engaged to be married. She looked happy for her sister, and strangely enough the news did nothing for Jim. He was glad that all the weeks of uncertainty were over. At last he knew where he stood. But he knew he had been a fool. All the years of searching for a soul mate and it had been there right under his nose. She had taken his heart long ago, and he would not admit it. The truth hit him for six and he whispered her name,

'Ann,' he said, 'when did you creep in and take my heart, and I was too blind to see?'

Chapter 15

When Jim told his mother, she was so happy. But she warned him, 'Be gentle and patient. Ann is loyal to her sister and shy. She will have to win her approval from Eileen before she gives herself to you. But she will.'

'You like her, don't you Mum?'

'Dear boy, I love her deeply. Why do you think I asked her here, in the first place?'

'That's good!' Jim gave a deep sigh.

The next time Ann went to see her sister, they discussed the watch. Eileen brought up the subject. 'I don't want to see it any more,' she told her.

Ann suggested they ask Bill Clarke to come to the cottage and see Jim and take a final decision, to which Eileen agreed.

'He stole it from a dead man, you know,' Eileen said. 'His widow Daisy should have it.'

'Who's been talking to you?' asked Ann. She looked at Eileen in surprise.

'Nobody. I've just been remembering a few things.' Eileen put her hands on her head. 'It's all up here in my memory. I only let it come out when I found the truth about Heinrich. He was a fake. His first trick was to disguise himself as a fisherman. I didn't see it. It was all so clever and a way to get here into the port to prepare for the invasion. It all came flooding back, Ann. My memory threw up a lot of backwash. I've been a fool. I've never really loved Jim or the

German, it's always been John Shaw,' she said sadly, looking at Ann for sympathy.

'Well. I've been in love with Jim for a long time. But you were in the way!'

'Oh! Ann, that's wonderful. I would be so happy to see you together.'

Ann bent over and hugged her sister. 'I have to go now, back to our place. It's been empty for a few days while I've been staying at Jim's cottage. It saves all that journey to and from work, but I don't like to leave it empty more than three days out of seven. Is there anything you want me to bring you from there?'

'No.' said Eileen. 'Give my bedroom a good clean for me and when you change the sheets, throw them out. I would sooner take two hospital bed sheets than sleep in them any more. But you wouldn't understand, my innocent little sister.'

'I think I might,' murmured Ann, looking at her sister with love and unshed tears.

When she reached number seven Glanmer Road, Ann noticed a light on inside, as she put her key in the lock. She walked through into the kitchen and was surprised to see Jim and Mrs Sharpe there, talking. Jim tried to look calm, but his heart was thumping. He needed to get Ann back to the Forest to Beech Cottage. He knew it was going to be difficult to explain to Ann, without telling her the truth. The truth would not only be frightening but would be breaking solemn vows. He must tell lies if necessary and say that his mother was unwell. But he must get her out of Southampton tonight.

They talked and at last Mrs Sharpe went home. Jim was left to press her to go with him. He nearly gave up after a while but one last plea and a mention of Mum being poorly and alone in the cottage, and Ann changed her mind.

'Yes! I can't leave Martha up there on her own. If she's not well, she needs me,' said Ann, gathering her things together.

'How we getting there?' she asked.

'Bill Clarke gave me a lift down in his sergeant's old car. I asked him to wait until you came back from the hospital, Ann. But we must go!'

They locked up the house and turned out the lights in the kitchen before they left. Bill Clarke was waiting. He made them get in quickly and was off. The usual guard at the top of the road was swigging at drink from a bottle. He seemed happy. 'I coaxed him off my back with a bottle of whisky,' said Bill.

They sped through Totton as it was clear but on reaching the edge of the Forest they were stopped by a German patrol. Bill told them that they were bringing his wife back home from Southampton Hospital. Ann tried to look frail and unwell and with her pale face, she looked the part, even though it was pale from fear and they were allowed to continue their journey.

Bill dropped Ann and Jim off at Wick Lane drove up the narrow unmade road to his own cottage in the woods, arriving with the last few drops of petrol in the tank. There was nothing he could do about that tonight, he thought grimly, in fact the situation would be no better in the morning since it was almost impossible to get petrol.

Jim opened the door with his key and was relieved to see his mother had gone to bed.

Ann said, 'Has she been in bed all day?'

'No,' said Jim, with his heart in his mouth. 'No, I took her up a drink of cocoa before I left.'

'But she has her bedside light out,' said Ann.

'Well, she must have felt better and settled. You go on in to bed. I'm just coming up. I shall tap your door if she calls in the night,' he said, remembering to look anxious.

'Goodnight, Jim, I'll be there if you need me.

'Goodnight, Ann. I knew you would.'

Before sleep overtook him, Jim had made plans for the waking hours. He vowed he would get that first cup of tea into his mother early in the morning, so he could have a little talk with her. Lies! She would kill him.

If he had left Ann on her own she would have been very frightened if the relief force had arrived and there had been shooting.

He woke early and made a pot of tea. There was no milk in the cool larder, so he hurried across the fields to the farm. Bill Webb was busy milking. He had milked his ten cows on his own now, as his only son, Andrew, had been called up for war service and had joined the army. Jim had remembered to bring a jug, and the milk was still warm, having not yet been through the cooler. He was in a hurry, but he waited long enough to hear the news. It had come from Bill's

180

brother, Percy, who lived in Southampton. A small contingent of the British army had marched down from several counties in the north and had circled Southampton. 'At five o'clock this morning,' he said, 'they were entering the north side, and meeting up with a company from Shrewsbury. That's it! All I know at the present time, Jim,' he said.

'Did you hear anything last night? asked Jim.

'No. Well, you wouldn't hear hand to hand fighting or small arms fire. Not this far away.'

Muttering grateful thanks, Jim hurried back to the cottage. Standing there in the blue and white kitchen, in her red flannel dressing gown was Ann, a worried look on her face. 'Jim, I wondered what was happening.'

'I only went across to the farm for some milk,' he said grinning. 'All hot, too! Straight from the cow.'

'How's Mum?'

'Just going up with her tea, so I'll find out,' he said, picking up his mother's cup. Ann took it from him. 'I'll take it up.'

Jim looked at her and decided it was no use in arguing. So be it! It seemed hours to Jim, waiting for Ann to return but of course she went in her bedroom and dressed before coming down again to the kitchen. When she did, she seemed happy.

'Martha is better; she thinks it was something she ate yesterday. She said the bread had green mildew on it.' Ann wrinkled up her nose as she spoke.

After breakfast, Jim took his ferrets out to the end of the long garden and picked up his nets. He put the ferrets in the holes, and sure enough they were in the burrows. He caught two rabbits and gave a sigh of relief. At least they would eat now. Ann loved rabbit stew. He hung them up in the larder. It was getting serious; the only other food in there was a lump of farm butter, a jug of milk and a crust of mildewy, stale bread. There was a large bag of flour, but not enough to start bread making on an every-day scale. He was afraid his mother would start making plans to go shopping. It was unsafe at the moment and Jim decided to tell the two women the situation.

Ann was busy cleaning the kitchen and Martha was dragging a large basket of logs in for the fire. The cottage was cold and she looked up when Jim called out.

'You don't have to work for the next three days, do you Ann?'

Surprised at his question, she said, 'No, you know Mr Dobbs only needs me four days a week. It leaves me three days off covering the weekend.'

'Well, from what I've heard, more of our own troop reinforcements have arrived at last to help defeat this invasion. They have already reached the outskirts of Southampton. The Home Guard and soldiers from the south coast have secured all of the roads leading through Forest. The Germans won't find it easy to get in there. Now how it is going to affect the people, the ones at work or in their homes I don't know.'

'How do you know all this?' asked Ann.

Jim's mother answered that one for him. 'He moves around and has mates in the Home Guard,' she said quietly and winked an eye at her son.

Ann's face was a mixture of utter amazement and admiration. She stared hard at Jim. 'Is that why you insisted I come back here with you and your Mum?'

'Yes. I hated myself for not telling you the truth, but Ann, I was under strict orders not to talk. I made a vow of silence.' After a moment more he said, 'I couldn't leave without you, Ann. You mean so much to me. I'm a blind fool. It's you I love and worry about. It has always been you.'

The room was hushed. No other words or conversation were necessary. Martha looked as if she had just won a thousand pounds. Ann, with tears of joy, ran across to Jim and he folded her in his arms. 'This is where you belong,' he whispered.

Ann was the first to break the silence. 'What about shopping for food?' She sounded more bewildered than afraid.

'The streets are dangerous. To be out at all is asking to be shot or taken hostage by the Germans which is worse,' said Jim, calmly but firmly. 'Everyone's been advised to stay in their own homes. Bolt the doors and keep away from the windows. And that's what we shall do!'

They stayed in Beech Cottage for two days, afraid to go outside the door. Martha said she could hear gunfire in the distance. Their neighbour Bill, who was brave enough to call in with fresh milk, told them the latest news that he had heard: The RAF were in control of the skies over the Channel once more and there were British warships in the Solent.

A detachment of British soldiers called on all the cottages in that area, to see they had food. They brought fresh bread from their camp. Ann was worried about Eileen and asked them if the hospital in Southampton was safe. 'It's my sister, Nurse Smith, who's a patient there. I haven't been able to get to see her.'

The soldier assured her that the patients and staff were all guaranteed their safety. 'As for Nurse Smith,' he said, 'she was flirting with half the British army!'

'Shows she's better, getting well again,' said Ann, with a wry smile.

Jim asked the men what Glanmere Road was like. 'Probably all right mate, said the sergeant. 'No windows were smashed. Hundreds of Germans have been taken prisoner while at their main camp on Southampton Common. All under canvas they were,' he said. 'Most of them asleep. We just killed the guards on duty first, no shots, just a knife in the neck.' The soldier paused for a brief moment. 'The rest was easy as our reinforcements have arrived. One of the Germans cursed Hitler. He said why didn't he send us more troops; there were not enough of us here.'

'He took a risk from his officers, opening his mouth like that,' said Jim.

The soldier smiled at Jim, and then he said calmly, 'Germany bit off more than it could chew. Now they've got the Russians on their back!'

The sergeant joined the rest of the detachment outside the cottage. They had been searching for one German who was known to have broken through the ring and was somewhere in the forest.

'There are traps that were set for that purpose,' said Jim. However, the soldiers knew and had a map of the dangerous places which were deep in the forest. They asked him how he came to know about traps but Jim simply told them that he was a forester, born and bred and knew every bush or blade of grass. He asked if it was safe to go into the town but they advised him not to do so until the all-clear sirens went. This was the army's plan. There were still a few Germans in hiding.

Jim asked if they had been to the nurseries in Wick Lane. The owner's house had been taken over, he told them. Mostly German officers.

The soldiers thanked Jim and went back to get reinforcements. There were not enough of them to take prisoners. They left some troops on guard around Wick Lane, until they came back.

Jim went back to the cottage. His mum was making a pot of tea. She watched as he drew the heavy curtains and bolted and locked the doors.

'What's up, Jim?' She spoke quietly in case Ann was within earshot. She didn't want to alarm her.

Jim looked his mum straight in the eye. 'We have to protect ourselves, not that we're in danger, we're not, but we need to be careful until they take the officers who are in Cliff Dobbs' house.

'Nice little hideaway. I knew about it, you know,' said Jim's mum, calmly.

He looked at her in surprise. 'How did you find out?' he asked.

'Well, dear, you remember the candles that night?'

'Yes,' Jim frowned. 'Yes, Cliff Dobbs came and wanted to borrow some candles. They had a power failure in the house. So what?'

'Well, I picked about three candles out of the box. Cliff said that will be fine, that is enough Martha. But the German officer who came with him wanted more. He said that they needed enough for the four bedrooms, also supper table, and your room. I remember thinking. Oh yes! You have a house full of guests Cliff. But why try to hide them? Unless of course they are Germans.'

Jim remained silent as she continued, 'I can see the house from my bedroom window through the net curtains. My nets are useful because they couldn't see me watching them,' said his mother with a satisfied smile on her face.

'You're a clever old thing'! Jim said, giving her a hug.

'I'm going on up to see what happens when they come for them.'

'It's too early for bed yet, Mum.'

'No! I'm not going to bed. I want to watch our boys catch them.'

'OK,' said Jim. 'Whatever you do, don't put a light on, and get well back from the window if they start shooting'.

At that moment Ann came from the kitchen. She had been cooking, having skinned the rabbit, cut it in pieces, washed it and left it in a basin of cold water. She had also made a tray of scones, which gave the little kitchen an appetising smell.

Martha kissed her on the cheek as she went by. 'Thank you, Ann, what a lovely surprise. My daughter has made us some scones Jim,' she said with a cheeky smile. Jim took Ann's hand and led her into the sitting room. Then he took her in his arms and kissed her. It was dark now, but he didn't put the lights on.

It was anything *but* a silent night. The Germans were taken prisoners and some shots were fired. Cliff Dobbs went all to pieces, unable to run the nurseries. Loyal Joe who had been employed there since Cliff started in 1936, worked on, running the greenhouses without pay, until Cliff was ready to work again.

It was nearing the end of the brief German occupation. They were outnumbered by British troops, more arriving from the north each day. Winchester and Romsey were free, as were countless other small towns surrounding the port of Southampton. The British army distributed food in the towns. They continued to bring fresh bread to the Foresters, who by now were killing their animals for food, the pigs, poultry, even their turkeys. The farmers and smallholders held a general meeting to discus a share basis, by which every family had food in a radius of so many miles. If they could pay for the food at a minimum cost, they would. The cottagers, who had no means to pay, were entered in the logbook under the title 'Gift'. As Bill Webb remarked, 'This is just for the emergency of the invasion, until there's time to reorganise the distribution of food in the area. In four weeks time, the Ministry of food will be on our backs, no doubt. But we are Foresters and can't let out neighbours starve. The situation at the moment is serious beyond measure. We're not allowed to kill our own cows. But I can send Snowdrop to the cattle market for slaughter. She might pass as table meat. The old bag is too old for her own good. I've had no milk from her for ages. The bull can't stand the sight of her, he walks away.'

Jim Blake looked at the farmer: He was wonderful! This whole thing was his idea and Jim was worried that his old friend could be putting his livelihood on the line, if the Ministry of Food and Fisheries came down on him later. He grinned across the room at Bill.

'Cheers,' he said, 'for taking the gloom from a meaty meeting, Bill. Trust you to see the funny side of life.' The old Forest pub shook with laughter.

The days went by and still the army had not cleared Southampton. A group of German soldiers had taken hostages: Three families near the old walls of Southampton had let the enemy into their houses. Cramped in a small space with old underground cellars, it was difficult to get them out. For one thing the soldiers were well armed, and threatened the household, children included. Finally though, one brave man had secured the released of the hostages. It had meant killing the Germans in each location, doing so in the only way he knew, with a knife in an artery in the neck. His theory had been that sooner or later they would have to sleep, a German is no different to anyone else; sleep will overtake the body and mind. Among other things he was a historian and had studied the Southampton Bargate. He knew the secret tunnels and cellars dotted among the remaining old walls of the town.

The first house containing the hostages was not easy but once inside, he hid and crept up behind the German soldier, who was selfishly eating the only scraps of food in the barricaded house. It was so swift and over in seconds. The German did not have time to reach for his gun.

The second house was easier and he went in the front door as a bearded, long-lost Uncle Ben. Once inside and after having a gun constantly prodding his back, he worked an old trick, 'There is someone behind you'. The German fell for it. He spun round firing his gun at the same time. Off guard, the frail old man who called himself Uncle Ben, killed him instantly with a knife in his neck artery.

The couple in the house with their one small child had behaved wonderfully, seeing through the unorthodox way of trying to rescue them from the German intruder. The woman of the house acted out the confrontation at the door better than a professional actress, hugging Uncle Ben and once inside even wept at his long awaited return. If it had not been both dangerous and risky it would have been funny, before the killing.

'I've never in my life seen an act so quickly. It was too fast for human vision,' the woman said. 'It was all over in a second.' The old man who had saved their lives pulled his beard off, and then his white eyebrows, then he took the padding from the back of his jacket, and lost his humped back. Then in a flash he was gone. The couple were left breathless, sad because they had no time to thank him and once more, no one knew his name.

The final rescue was the last: Two Germans had been holding a young family hostage in a flat above a baker's shop for two days. The unknown man had a long talk with the army, who were most reluctant to let him rescue the family. First, they demanded to know who he really was, seeing he was not in army uniform.

The army Captain thanked him for his help in the last two rescues, but warned of the danger of this one. He said, 'I don't wish to reveal my real name. Call me Mike. You see I am a member of one of the Auxiliary Units, and the Secret Army.'

'Ah! So that is it? You trained with my unit in Coleshill. Right then, Mike, it's your decision. I can't send you in. What are your plans?'

'Stay in the bakery for a while. They'll get hungry and there's plenty of bread down in the shop. I worked here as a fourteen-year-old boy, so I know there's a tiny staircase in a cupboard behind the bread shelf. It was used many years ago, as they kept the grain in a room upstairs and ground it by hand. They have to sleep, so I shall go in at night. If you hear a shot, then I need help. I think there are two Germans in there. Don't wait for the second shot.'

The Captain shook his hand. 'Good luck, Mike.'

Two days later it was all over. The Germans turned their guns on themselves, but not before they had shot and wounded Mike. The family were all safe, huddled together in a little cupboard, sitting on stairs white with dust and cobwebs.

Mike kept the news of his wounds in his side to himself. He asked the soldiers who took the German bodies away if they could take him home at once. The Captain was there and took him.

'Where do you live, mate?'

'The New Forest. I'll show you the way,' he said grimly.

'You all right?' The Captain looked at him and noticed blood on his sleeve. 'I had better get you to the hospital.'

'No! You will do me the kindness please of taking me home. Here we are. This is it,' he said softly.

'But this is the forest. I don't see any houses,' said the Captain, 'only trees.'

'Oh, they are there, all right. Now let me out, Sir.'

'OK, but I don't like this, Mike, and this is only woods!'

Mike got out of the car, drawing on all the strength he had left. 'Goodbye, Sir. This is my home. My name, by the way, is Ray Wicks, Auxiliary Secret Army. Keep it my secret, you will if you are a gentleman. I was born here in the Forest and I will die in it. It's God's Country.'

The Captain drove away, much against his will, but he had to. It was a very brave man's death wish.

Chapter 16

It had been the most silent night since the invasion. Not a sound, not a shot fired but the peace was broken at six-thirty in the morning by the wailing sound of an air raid clear. It seemed strange after such a long time. There had been no enemy aircraft over Southampton for quite a while.

Jim went into Ann's bedroom first, then into his mother's. 'They've gone,' he said, 'the Germans are gone! Our troops took most of them prisoners. I was told by an army officer that when the last one was taken, the All Clear Siren would be sounded.'

'That's it?'

'Mum, that's it! Jim ran back to Ann's bedroom. 'Will you marry me, Ann? Please say yes.'

'Well, at least let me put my dressing gown on, Jim!' He laughed and he grabbed her to him. 'Yes! Of course I will,' she said between laughter and tears of joy.

Jim's mum hovered in the doorway. 'I'm so happy for you. This is the happiest day of my life. I love you both,' she said, tears of a mother's love running down her cheeks.

'Hang on, you two,' Jim said, 'the Occupation may be finished but the war's not over yet! We do have difficult times ahead, don't forget.'

They went downstairs to breakfast, happy, but a little apprehensive, wondering what tomorrow would bring. Revenge air raids again? Later in the morning neighbours came in to see Martha. A pot of tea and Ann's scones were on the kitchen table. Chairs were pulled out and the women sat talking, unloading the pain and fear inside them.

Jim took Ann in to Southampton to see Eileen in the hospital. On their last visit she had been walking a few steps. When they left, Martha told her friends that Ann would soon be her daughter-in-law. Jim had proposed. There were genuine cries of delight for their old neighbour and friend.

'I haven't seen my Bill since yesterday morning,' said Ethel Clarke. 'I wish he hadn't joined that bloomin' Home Guard. He goes off, I don't know where, and I'm left sleeping on my own,' she said.

The farmer's wife looked at her and shook her head. 'You don't know what it's like to be a farmer's wife, Ethel, my Bill is never in. He is midwife to his cows, slave to his pedigree pigs, and never takes me out.'

'Oh dear, poor Mrs Clarke,' said Martha, filling her cup with fresh tea. 'What you need is a short piece of string, and a belt.'

Rays' wife, Doris, sat very quietly. She did not join in the happy laughter. Martha had noticed how withdrawn she was, though she had smiled and thanked Martha for the tea, and scone. 'Would you like another scone? My future daughter-in-law made these last evening,' she asked.

'No thank you, Martha. My Ray has been gone four days and nights now. I'm getting a bit worried. I don't know where he is.'

'Don't worry, Doris.' Ethel put her hand across the table and took her hand. 'Your husband and mine are Home Guard. They have their duty like a soldier. I expect they're in Southampton or on the fringe of the Forest. We should be grateful, as they have been protecting us. Ray was the leader too. You should be proud of him.'

A sudden tap on her door made Martha jump. She opened her cottage door and found Cliff Dobbs standing there.

'Come in, Cliff.'

He smiled and greeted the ladies warmly. 'I've come to see Ann,' he said to Martha. 'I can take her on full-time now. The nursery's going to be busy soon once the railway's open and we can get stuff up to Covent Garden.'

'Well, Cliff, I'm afraid they are not here at the moment. Ann and Jim have gone to Southampton to see her sister, Eileen.'

'Ann's sister! I don't know which is which. They are really an eye catcher. I've never seen any like it.'

'They're identical twins, Cliff. One fertilised egg split in half, so I've been told,' Martha said with a grin. 'I'll tell Ann when she comes in, that you have been. I daresay she will help you out.'

He thanked Martha for the offer of tea and scone and hurried back. There was so much to do now. 'You are certainly looking a lot better after your break,' she called after him.

'Yeah! I'm better now them bloody Germans are gone,' he shouted as he shut the little gate. Martha went back to her guests.

When they were gone she cleared away the cups and put some more coal on the fire that Jim had lit before he left.

Her thoughts were on Jim for the rest of the morning. Would he be pulled by emotion again, back into Eileen's trap? He had Ann there with him, and there was no doubt that he loved her. The two girls were not identical characters. Ann was softer but her sister had a magnetic personality. Men were drawn to her. They could never say no to her. She enjoyed flirting.

Martha prayed that her son could be strong. She didn't want Eileen as a daughter-in-law but her son was a softie, a tender-hearted man. He could be won over. She gave herself a mental shake. 'Stop it!' she said out loud. She put the cup on the wooden draining board so sharply that she chipped the china rim. 'Now look what you've done,' she muttered to herself. 'You silly old woman.'

It was a pleasant evening: After supper they sat around the fire. It was still chilly, but lighter evenings were approaching. At six-thirty it was still light, and they had yet another visitor: Bill Clarke came to see Jim. They talked for a while on family matters then he asked Jim how Eileen was progressing.

'Eileen is doing fine,' said Jim. 'We went to see her this morning.'

'Yes! She's walking now. Only we went too far up the corridor and Jim had to carry her back in his arms. She hasn't got a lot of strength yet,' said Ann.

'Where is her doctor? That Doctor Shaw she is engaged to now?' said Martha, quick as a flash.

'You know Eileen; she has cooled off a bit. He wanted her to get married straight away. It was too soon,' said Ann, with a sigh.

'Well, Jim, I hear from my wife that you two are an item. Ethel said you and Ann are engaged. Martha told her this morning.'

'Yes! That's right,' said Ann.

'When is the happy day for you two?'

'Not just yet,' said Ann. 'Eileen said we should not rush things, especially in war time.'

'But then, you're not in the forces Jim,' said his mum.

Bill Clarke flashed a look at Martha. 'I'm sorry, but I came here to see Jim on his own. It's private, I'm afraid. Sorry!'

'That's all right; we'll go upstairs, Bill. There is something I want to give Ann.'

When they were alone, Jim spoke first. 'It's bad news, isn't it, Bill? I have that feeling.'

'Yes! I hate this job. They found Ray Wicks' body in the forest about an hour ago. He'd been shot. They said he bled to death. I think he just curled up and waited to die. Do you know, Jim, he looked so peaceful on the soft undergrowth. There were fresh deer droppings nearby. He must have felt the animal's breath on him, as it left a little trail of blood on its hoofs along a path. The two soldiers picked it up and followed the trail back to the body.'

Jim found it difficult to speak. He was choked. This had been his closest friend, his mate. 'You said soldiers! Did

Germans shoot him in the forest? They say there were two at large.'

'Look, Jim. We don't know. The army sent about thirty of their best men to clean the forest and make it safe for us. They went in about one o'clock and there are no Germans in there. '

'And they found the body about an hour ago?'

'Leave it, Jim!'

'We may never know what happened.'

It was dark, so Jim lit the lamp and pulled the curtains across. The women's voices got louder; they were coming down the stairs.

'One thing before you go, Bill. What do you think about this?' Jim held the watch in his hand. The first thing Bill did was open up the back.

'If it says George, Fred and William, I know who it belonged to,' he said. 'Yes! No doubts at all. It was Eric Small's watch. Jim, that was his three brothers who were all killed in the First War. He was only a little boy, there were many years between them but he adored them. You know, he had this made for him? Did you see the number eleven on the face?'

'No,' said Jim.

'Well, you look. There is a tiny cross with three golden dots. One dot for each brother.'

'Why number eleven, I wonder?' asked Jim.

'On the eleventh hour of the eleventh month – we remember them. Armistice Day.' Bill said sadly.

'Oh my God! What do we do?' said Jim.

'Give it to his widow, Daisy. But where did you get it?'

'It was among Eileen's things. She had an affair with Heinrich Shultz. He was killed in the Southampton train disaster. Someone put explosive on the railway line.'

'Yes! So they did!' Bill smiled and a strange look came on his face. 'So they did, by Jove!'

A couple of weeks after Ray Wicks' funeral Martha decided to cook a celebration meal for Jim and Ann. They had been to Romsey the previous day and bought the rings. It seemed a good time to buy her wedding ring as well, which pleased Jim's mother.

She also invited the two widows. Doris didn't know Daisy, but Martha wanted Ray Wicks' wife Doris to come out of her lonely cottage for a few hours. Her grief was pitiful.

Daisy Small had been widowed at the beginning of December, so it was only three months ago. Jim wanted to give her the watch that had once belonged to her late husband, Eric. It would be a powerful moment, but a happy one, too.

Jim went in to Southampton where she lived and brought her back her to Beech Cottage. He suggested to his mother that Ethel and Bill Clarke might come as well, as Eric had been his friend for many years and Martha had agreed, delighted.

'My Ann will help me cook the dinner. In fact I will kill two of my old hens for roasting. Mr Webb is sending me up a jug of milk, and a jug of cream, and some butter.'

There were seven at the table in the end, not eight as planned, all enjoying roast chicken. Eileen should have come, she was invited, but the night before she had sent a message with one of the nurses at the hospital. Martha gave the envelope containing the message to Ann who opened it, said nothing and passed it to Jim, who also read it and said nothing.

It was thrown on the table, while Jim and Ann were laughing together over an old photo of Jim as a boy.

'Well! What is in the message?' asked Jim's mum.

'Read it yourself,' said Jim, in a cool detached voice.

Martha unfolded the single sheet of paper. Her hands were trembling a little. The handwriting was clear if a bit unsteady. It simply said: 'Dear Ann, Sorry unable to come to the cottage for dinner. Thank Mrs Blake.

John and I got married yesterday in Registry Offices. Matron gave me away. Nurse Roper was witness. We are now on our way to Scotland for honeymoon. See you soon. Love, Eileen. (Mrs Shaw!)'

Martha smiled to herself. She, too, said nothing, except perhaps, 'Good!' Under her breath.

Jim's mother certainly put a lovely meal on the table. Her guests enjoyed their dinner, and the old hens turned out to be much more tender meat than she expected. There was much laughter and teasing about the roast chicken.

After everyone had finished Martha cleared the table and Ann and Jim did the washing up of the dishes, pots and baking tray. Then Jim pulled a circle of chairs around the open fire and when they had settled down, he told them he had something rather special to say.

The friendly chatter ceased when he came in and sat down. Each one was wondering what Jim had to say, and most of all what the little box contained that he was holding so carefully in his hand.

'Right!' he said, breaking the silence. 'Now I am going to present a treasure to someone here, who thought they had lost it forever. My hope now is that this article will make the person happy.' Jim's face was filled with emotion as he continued. 'This was stolen and has been through many hands before mine. But it is now going home, to its rightful owner. Daisy Small, here is your late husband Eric's watch. Unspoiled, in good working order, and where he would want it to be.' He got up from his armchair and went across to Daisy and handed her the little box containing the gold watch then he stumbled back to his armchair with tear-filled eyes, watching her take the lid off the box and gently taking out her Eric's watch. Her hands trembled so much it tapped against the cardboard box, so she had to use both her hands to hold it. Daisy closed her eyes and held it on her cheek. She couldn't speak. She couldn't get up out of the chair but she could move her arm, so she held out her hand towards Jim.

He got up and took it, and she pressed his hand against her wet cheek, while she mouthed the words, 'Thank you!'

Jim's mother broke the tension and got up. 'Right, my dears, this calls for a nice cup of tea.' With a bright smile, she went out into the kitchen. Ann got up and followed her.

Over a cup of tea Jim told the story of the watch. He left out the dark side of the story where Eileen had an affair with the thief, but felt it was suffice to say that he, Heinrich, brought her safely back from the hospital one night, did some odd jobs for her like getting coal in for her fire, washed his hands and forgot to put his watch back on.

'He was killed the following day.'

Ethel Clarke looked up at Jim. 'Didn't Eileen go on the train with that German?'

Jim's inside turned over, but loyal to the end, he said, 'She was supposed to go with me, but of course she didn't know that I was taken off that run. I tried to let her know in time, but couldn't, so she went on her own.'

'Oh!' Ethel Clarke seemed satisfied and the conversation turned to other subjects. The invasion was over, but the war still raged on. The Germans had started their bombing raids again but though they were just as dreadful as before, people were less apprehensive about their significance. Hitler wouldn't launch another invasion again for a long time, perhaps not ever!

Ann and Jim drew closer together as the weeks flew by. Their love turned to passion and Jim found the shy girl had a spark of fire that he did not know. It became difficult to live under the same roof with a third party.

Martha knew this and was so happy for them. It came as a relief to her when Jim said to his mum one morning, 'We're going ahead now. We can't wait any longer, we are tying the knot.'

'Good!' said his mother. 'When?'

'Well, we are getting married next Saturday,' said Jim. 'We have been making arrangements now for some time. Ann wants to be married in the little church in Southampton where her mother was wed to her dad, Harry.' He hesitated for a moment. 'You don't mind, Mum?'

Martha beamed at him as she said, 'Of course not. I think it's lovely. Is she having a white dress, son?'

'No, Mum. It's going to be simple; you see we need to save what little money we have for our future home. Eileen and John will come, but will go back to Scotland after the wedding. They have decided to live there and make Scotland their home. John has been offered a good job in the hospital there. And of course, as she said, his parents are there in Scotland.'

'Where will you live?' Martha clutched the edge of the kitchen table as she spoke.

'We are buying Eileen's half of the house her mother left them,' said Jim. 'She has said they don't want it. We'll stay here for a while if we may, until it's settled.'

'Of course, Jim. I had hoped you would. You and Ann can have the front large bedroom and I will go into your room at the back.'

Jim looked at his mother and was touched. 'No! You won't go moving anywhere, Mum. Ann and I can manage quite well in the back room.' He went across and hugged her.

'Go on with you,' she murmured, 'I'll give you all the privacy you want.'

'Well, Ann will talk to you when she comes in,' he said with a grin.

It was a typical first of May Day with blustery wind and an occasional shower. Not all that warm, but nothing could spoil the joy in their hearts as they exchanged vows in the shabby, war-marked church. Jim felt his heart would burst with pride.

The twin sisters looked so lovely and the bond that had always tied them was still visible.

Jim took first place today and could only see one. Mrs Sharpe and George, her son, had done a lot of work on the little house. Number seven was to be their honeymoon house. Dear old Mrs Sharpe had got it all ready for them.

It was still war time and travelling was not easy. The little house was a perfect hideaway for a week. A week together to unfold their love, a love so deep and so binding, a love with passion and fire.

The moment of sadness came when the girls had to part. Ann watched with tears in her eyes when Eileen and John drove away. Ann knew she would not see her sister for a very long time. Scotland was a long way from Southampton. They had never been far apart before. They had been very close as sisters.

Then she turned and Jim was by her side. She looked deep into his eyes. 'Eileen has gone,' she whispered, 'you have chosen the right one.' Her words hung for a second like a question in the still evening air.

Jim cupped her beautiful face with his hands before he closed his lips on hers. 'My darling, precious wife,' he said softly, 'I am going to spend my life proving it to you.'